MURDER TOO LATE

Murder Too Late

A Patrick Dawlish Mystery

John Creasey *writing as* Gordon Ashe

ISBN: 978-1-5040-9813-7

This edition published in 2025 by Open Road Integrated Media, Inc.
180 Maiden Lane
New York, NY 10038
www.openroadmedia.com

MURDER TOO LATE

Chapter 1

WELCOME GUESTS

Dawlish put his head round the window of the dining-room where Felicity, his wife, was putting the finishing touches to the table. She was preoccupied with two small vases, which were over-flowing with roses, too long stemmed, too top heavy for their containers.

The clock struck six.

"How's progress?" asked Dawlish.

Felicity jumped. "Pat! You scared me."

"Sorry, my sweet," apologised Dawlish, "I thought you heard me coming."

"These *won't* go right," Felicity said, distractedly. "Something always goes wrong at the last moment—and I haven't started to change."

"They'll love you for what you are, not for what you'll look like," Dawlish murmured, and climbed through the window. To Felicity's alarm, he began to fiddle with one of the vases, and immediately three of the roses fell out. "Well, would you believe that?" asked Dawlish, in dismay.

Felicity took him firmly by the arm.

"I would indeed, now if you really want to help," she suggested, "you could pick a few eating apples. There are plenty on the trees at the end of the orchard. And then, do go and change. There's no reason why you shouldn't be ready in time, even if I'm not."

Dawlish grinned, and lifting her bodily, for he was a large man, kissed the end of her nose. Next moment he was out of the window, striding across the lawn. The early evening sun shone on his crisp, fair hair, his pleasant, though undistinguished features, which gave little indication of his flair for criminology.

At the archway leading to the orchard, he turned and waved.

Felicity turned back to the roses. They would do as they were, she decided. She surveyed the table, which was set for six—the Dawlish's and four guests. The sun shone on cut glass, on silver and highly polished wood. Felicity was satisfied, and went out, humming under her breath.

In the kitchen Chloe, the cook-general and the only servant who lived in, looked up with a broad smile.

"Everything's going just right, ma'am, thanks to Mrs. Arbor here."

A little, skinny woman who was peeling potatoes, simpered self-consciously.

"I'm sure I'm glad to help."

"We couldn't have managed without you," Felicity assured her, "I won't interfere then, Chloe."

"We'll be ready at half-past seven to the tick," Chloe asserted, "and it's a lovely bird."

"I've never seen a better," volunteered Mrs. Arbor fulsomely, "not even at Christmas."

Felicity eased herself gently out of a situation of thanks and congratulations that Mrs. Arbor obviously intended to prolong indefinitely, and hurried upstairs to change.

From the bedroom window, she caught sight of Dawlish

half-way down the orchard. He was not hurrying. Smoke was curling from his pipe, and once he stopped to look over the countryside which stretched beyond *Four Ways*, their Surrey home. He could see Alum village, nearly a mile away in one direction, and Haslemere in the other. The evening was warm, the sky was a gentle, pleasing blue. The guests were due 'about seven' and as Tim Jeremy was driving, that probably meant a quarter past.

"I'll have to hurry," murmured Felicity.

The apples picked, Dawlish strolled back across the lawn. *Four Ways* was a modern house; it looked modern; it made no pretence to an earlier period, and yet it merged with the countryside perfectly. The gardens were nearly matured; another three or four years would bring them to perfection. When he and Felicity had decided to live in the country, they had dreamed of something like *Four Ways* and, lo! their dream had come true.

The village church clock struck the half-hour. He quickened his step, and soon reached the back of the house. By the kitchen window, Mrs. Arbor was preparing a cauliflower.

"Apples as requested," said Dawlish, and put them on the window sill. "How are things going?"

"Lovely!" exclaimed Mrs. Arbor, "I've never seen a better bird . . ."

Upstairs, Dawlish found his evening clothes, his white tie, neatly laid out.

After dinner, they were to go into Haslemere for *the* ball of the summer season. It was a charity ball, and all Surrey and his wife would be there.

Dawlish changed.

He was just putting the finishing touches to his tie when the telephone rang. There was an extension in the bedroom. Felicity called out "I wonder who *that* is, I do hope nothing's delayed them."

"Stop worrying," Dawlish lifted the receiver. "Hallo—Dawlish speaking."

"Hallo, Pat," said a voice which was familiar but which Dawlish did not immediately place. "Is that invitation still open?"

"I don't know," said Dawlish, trying to think who it was. "What's it to and when—"

"Dinner tonight, for Grace and—"

"Bill!" exclaimed Dawlish.

"Certainly it's Bill! We did say no, but if you can manage it, I'd be grateful."

Dawlish heard a subdued argument, and then a woman's voice sounded loudly in his ear.

"Major Dawlish, I've told Bill that he wants shooting! It's impossible for us to spring ourselves on you at the last minute. We'll be seeing you at the ball, and—"

"Do hold on, I won't keep you a second." Dawlish placed a hand over the mouthpiece, and called: "Fel—can we squeeze Bill and Grace in?"

There was a pause, and then: "The Trivetts?"

"Yes."

"I—" began Felicity, and appeared in the doorway, in a diaphanous negligee which concealed very little. She was frowning, but suddenly her face cleared. "Well—yes, darling, of course."

Dawlish took his hand away.

"Felicity says that it's a lovely bird, and it'll be no trouble at all."

"But we *can't*—" began Grace.

"Give me that telephone," insisted Bill Trivett. There was a pause; then: "Hallo, Pat. You're sure it's not putting you out?"

"Yes, of course. Can you be here by half-past seven?"

"On the dot," promised Trivett. "I particularly want a chat with you before the ball."

"Mixing business with pleasure?" asked Dawlish absently, and Felicity, still standing in the doorway, stiffened. "May you be forgiven." He replaced the receiver, thoughtfully. Felicity approached from behind, and touched his shoulder.

"Pat," said Felicity.

"My sweet, you'll catch your death!"

"Don't prevaricate," Felicity said impatiently. "Is Bill coming to talk business?"

"How should I know? But I should say not. I gathered that their arrangements had fallen through and they're all dressed up with nowhere to dine, so—"

"I don't believe it," said Felicity, adding illogically: "How like a policeman to spoil my dinner party!"

Dawlish looked shocked. "A policeman? Superintendent William Trivett of New Scotland Yard!"

"Still a policeman," insisted Felicity. She stood for a moment without moving. For the first time that day her eyes looked troubled; there was no telling what Dawlish would do, or what Trivett might ask him to do. For Dawlish was a man who revelled in adventure, and Felicity often wished he were not.

A long, shrill blast on a car horn startled them both.

"Heavens! They're here already!" cried Felicity distractedly.

"Do go down to them, I won't be five minutes!" She picked up her lipstick. Dawlish grinned and kissed her. She pushed him away, Trivett's call forgotten in her haste, and Dawlish hurried downstairs.

Chloe, neat in black and white, and looking as if her only task was to let the guests in, was standing in the hall. Outside, advancing towards the front door, was a tall, thin, good-looking man—Timothy Jeremy—and another, as tall, but fatter; he was Ted Beresford. Joan Beresford was a small woman, especially when compared with her husband, and the only stranger, in whose honour Felicity had made so much fuss, was Anne Grayson, a girl of medium height, very dark and easy to look at. She was by Tim's side; the Dawlish's had heard much about Tim's young woman.

Dawlish greeted them on the porch.

"Don't let his size scare you," comforted Tim, taking her elbow. "He's really quite tame."

"And moderately well-trained," observed Beresford.

They filled the hall. Dawlish held Joan Beresford's hand for a moment, and told her that she looked more lovely than ever. Then:

"Will you look after Anne? Felicity had a last minute rush, but she won't be long. The usual room."

Joan led Anne off.

Dawlish told the men to help themselves to drinks while he rushed to the dining table to lay the extra places for the Trivetts.

Back in the drawing-room he found Beresford hovering over the array of bottles.

"What's it to be?" he asked Dawlish.

"Whisky," said Dawlish, and Beresford, who did not need telling how his host liked it, finished his job. They stood by the open French windows, looking onto lawns and flower-beds, and Beresford turned and grinned at Dawlish.

"You're a lucky dog," he said.

"As for luck, or should I say good fortune," murmured Dawlish, "you aren't doing so badly."

"I've no complaints," Beresford assured him. His smile, showing excellent white teeth, relieved his face of ugliness.

Beresford moved to a chair and sat on the arm a little stiffly.

It was three months since either he or Jeremy had been to *Four Ways*, although Dawlish had met them fairly frequently in London; but it would not greatly matter if they did not see one another for years on end, their bond of friendship being strong enough to withstand separation. Perhaps it was because of Trivett's telephone call that his mind was running on the past—on the times when they had worked together in affairs of violence, such as the time when Beresford had lost his leg.

Beresford looked at him quizzically.

"Dark thoughts, Pat?"

"Distracted ones. Bill Trivett and his wife are coming over."

Jeremy rubbed his hands together. "Splendid!"

"I thought you said he couldn't make it," said Beresford.

"He's changed his mind. I rather think the idea is to mix business with pleasure," murmured Dawlish.

They eyed him with sudden alertness.

"What's that?" asked Jeremy.

"That's all I know. When we first asked them he said he couldn't make it. Then he rang up half an hour ago to see if we could squeeze him in. It had a slightly depressing effect on Felicity, but she rallied. How much of your dark past does Anne know, Tim?"

"Most of it," Jeremy informed him.

"How does it affect her?"

"It intrigues," said Jeremy.

Beresford rubbed the back of his neck.

"Let's not start imagining ambiguous motives in Bill's visit. Didn't he give you any idea what he wanted?"

"No more than I've told you."

"He probably needs a spot of help," said Jeremy, lazily. "I always told him he'd never be able to rest until he'd persuaded you to join the C.I.D."

"Heaven forbid," protested Beresford.

"Leave that to Felicity," murmured Dawlish, dryly, and finished his drink. "Anyhow, I've grown fond of the quiet life."

"The great Patrick turned fruit-farmer," grinned Jeremy.

"And I'll have you know that I made thirty pounds out of the Bramleys, nearly fifty out of the soft fruit, and if it hadn't been for the late frost, the strawberries would have yielded another fifty," Dawlish announced with some pride. "It's only a matter of fighting a different kind of pest," he added, "and—but that's enough, here come the girls."

"And here, if I'm not mistaken," said Beresford, glancing out of the window, "comes Bill Trivett."

Chapter 2

BUSINESS AND PLEASURE

The Trivett's car passed through Haslemere at a speed too great to be entirely seemly for a policeman. For the most part his wife sat silent, watching the flashing countryside. Now and again she looked at her husband, knowing that he was not thinking about her.

"How much further is it?" she asked.

"Eh? Oh, a couple of miles," said Trivett, as if he had only then remembered that he was not alone. "Warm enough?"

"Yes."

He glanced at her, a little troubled.

"You needn't worry," he said, "Pat and Felicity Dawlish won't mind."

"If a couple descended on my dinner party at a moment's notice, I should mind exceedingly," said Grace. "They won't *say* we're nuisances, but—"

Trivett took one hand off the wheel, and lightly patted her knee.

"Forget it."

"Darling," said Grace, "putting business before pleasure is all right with me. I'm used to it. But when it comes to worrying others—"

"Dawlish is different from most others," Trivett reminded her.

"He's probably wishing you to perdition. He's settled down at his fruit farming, and—"

"Is longing for something else to do," Trivett assured her. "I know Pat."

"You haven't seen him for six months."

"He wouldn't change in sixty years!"

They fell silent as they passed through the village, a pleasant place, with a few thatched cottages and an oak-beamed inn. Not until they were climbing the road to *Four Ways* did either of them speak again; it was the moment when Beresford had seen the car from the sitting-room window.

"Why must it be Dawlish?" asked Grace.

"You know as well as I do," said Trivett. "He's got that something which makes him just the man for a job like this. Confound it, I'm not going to ask him to do much, just keep an eye on one or two people and let me know whether he thinks they're worth attention."

"And you're hoping he will do a lot more than keep an eye on them," suggested Grace dryly.

"No, I'm not. I value his opinion," Trivett said virtuously. "Outside the Yard, there isn't a man with Dawlish's qualifications, and—but you know that as well as I do."

"By the time this evening's over," predicted Grace, "we're going to be anathema to Felicity." After a pause, she added: "Is that the house?"

"Yes," said Trivett. "It looks attractive, doesn't it?"

"Very, but Dawlish wouldn't have retired here if he'd wanted a lot of excitement."

Trivett gave it up.

"All right, all right. We're going to make ourselves thoroughly unpopular, and before the night's out you're going to feel that Felicity wishes us to Kingdom Come. Dawlish is going to refuse to help, and we're going to spoil an evening that could have been good fun."

He drove in silence until he reached the gate of a drive cut into steep banks. The drive was winding, and fruit trees lined it—some well-established, others new since Dawlish had bought the house. Grace put a hand on his knee.

"Sorry," she said.

Trivett looked at her quickly.

"Shall I drop it?" he asked.

"No, go ahead—you wouldn't have gone to this trouble if you hadn't thought it necessary."

Dinner was over. From the first moment, everything had gone right, and Chloe had done the work of three. The women were upstairs, putting the finishing touches to their hair and make-up; three cars were standing outside, to take them into Haslemere. No one had as yet commented on Trivett's 'businesss'. Tim Jeremy, who had a droll humour not far removed from sardonic, had been the star of the evening. Now the four men were sitting about the drawing-room, Beresford and Dawlish smoking pipes, the others cigars.

A companionable silence was broken at last by Dawlish, who looked meaningly at Trivett. "Well, Bill, what's the guilty secret?"

Trivett grinned.

"Not particularly guilty, nor, by your expression, particularly secret. Merely that I thought you might be able to give us a spot of help."

"I knew it," said Jeremy, in a deep voice.

"Active or passive?" asked Dawlish.

"All three of us?" asked Beresford, hopefully.

"That's up to you, but it starts with Pat," said Trivett. "There isn't a great deal to go on—"

Trivett looked at each man in turn. He had worked with them on several cases before, through a little known Department of Intelligence. He had also worked with them on affairs into which Dawlish had jumped with both feet but, as he always declared, without knowing what he was doing. He had often maintained that he had not the slightest desire to emulate the police; and that was sincere enough, up to a point. After his last involvement in a couple of mysteries which had engaged the attention of the police and the interest of the press; he had said firmly that he was going to retire to grow fruit trees and rear a family.

Trivett, a shrewd judge of men, averted that Dawlish possessed a sixth sense in matters of deduction.

"Well?" asked Dawlish.

Trivett said: "It's as simple as this. We've had a lot of jewel robberies recently, not only in London but in the Home Counties. Some of them have been straightforward enough, and half a dozen of the cracksmen are now inside, but several are still out. We want to get them."

Dawlish nodded.

"I'm always reluctant to admit that there might be an organisation backing thieves," Trivett went on, slowly. "Most of the burglaries are done by men who make their living at it, few of them trust others, most of them work on their own or in little groups. But there's an indication that we've got something tougher to crack this time. We've recovered some of the jewels, but the rest of the stuff has totally disappeared. Some of it's good stuff. It doesn't seem to be on the market anywhere. The theory is that someone with a big collection is buying. If we're right, he might flood the market suddenly, or he might be smuggling the stuff abroad, or he might be keeping it for his own collection. The fact is that we can't find it through the normal channels, and it's worrying not only the Yard but the Home Office."

Dawlish nodded.

"We're being prodded all round," Trivett went on. "The insurance companies are protesting with vigour, and one way, and another, we've got our hands full. And if that isn't enough, one of the victims was knocked about pretty badly, three days ago. He died this afternoon."

"Making it murder," murmured Beresford. The three men were eyeing Trivett with deep interest.

"All this is straightforward police stuff," Dawlish said, slowly. "You're not so hard up for men that you want help from us, surely."

"If it weren't for one thing, we could manage well enough on our own. As it is, I've been given permission to talk to you about it."

Dawlish smoothed the bridge of his nose.

"So this is official?"

"Oh, yes." Trivett smiled. "And urgent, because we've had several pointers to one man, who lives not far from here and will be at the show tonight. All Surrey will be, including the Chief Constable," Trivett added. "And most of the women will be wearing all they've got in the way of jewellery. I'm rather expecting trouble tonight. It wouldn't altogether surprise me if there's a real attempt at a big coup. Still, I thought tonight would be a good chance for you to meet our suspect. You could follow up the acquaintance, and work from the inside, as it were. Any objections?"

"I could try," Dawlish said.

Trivett smiled with relief.

"That's fine! For all I know, you might know the man we've

got in mind. Sir Brian Alderney." He uttered the name slowly, as if he knew that it would cause a stir; and he watched Dawlish closely.

But it was Beresford who exclaimed: "My dear chap! You're crazy!"

"I know Alderney's got a good reputation," Trivett said, "and we haven't much to work on, but—well, we've some grounds for suspecting that he makes his money in curious ways. Do you know him, Pat?" He sat up. "What are you smirking like that for?" he demanded, testily.

Dawlish's smirk became a broad smile.

"Sorry. I was thinking of Felicity. The Big Noise on the committee running the ball tonight is Lady Alderney. Quite a charmer, and Felicity is by way of being a fellow committee member. I haven't met Lady Alderney or her husband, but I understand they're not only well-known and popular, but very well liked."

"Is there any real evidence?" Jeremy asked.

"Yes," said Trivett, "there's—"

"Here they come!" exclaimed Beresford, getting up slowly.

"Ted, take Felicity and Grace, will you?" asked Dawlish.

"Tim will take Anne, and Bill can drive me. I'll tell you all about it later. It's all right," he added, for Trivett's benefit, "Fel knows that something's brewing." He jumped up as the door opened and the four women came in, and looked at them, smiling. "*Quite* the belles of the ball," he said, "it's hardly fair."

"And what is that?" demanded Grace absently.

"Four such lovelies in one party," Dawlish said, "All ready?" He told them what they had arranged, watching Felicity a little anxiously. She showed no sign of annoyance. He helped her into the car, and whispered:

"I'll report faithfully when we get back."

"You'll tell Trivett it can't be done," said Felicity forcefully; but as she got into the car, she smiled.

On the journey Trivett admitted that the evidence against Alderney was slim; it amounted, in fact, to little more than indications. He was fabulously rich, a comparatively rare thing for a man of young middle age who had not inherited his wealth. There was mystery about his early life, which had been spent mostly in the Dominions. Fairly recently he had bought *Akers*, a big house between Haslemere and Godalming, not far from the Devil's Punch Bowl, commanding wonderful views over the Surrey countryside.

He was known to collect precious stones.

He was also known to have bought several jewels from doubtful sources; the police had actually interviewed him about them, and he had professed himself shocked that the man from whom he had bought them was a fence.

"For a man of the world, he protested a little too much," Trivett said. "To hear him talk, you'd think he'd never realised that there were such creatures as receivers of stolen goods in the world. The impression I got was that he was laughing up his sleeve."

"You didn't interview him, did you?" asked Dawlish, quickly.

"Indeed, no! I wouldn't be with you tonight if I had. The local people saw him—do you know young Leven?"

"No."

"He's a useful chap," Trivett said. "Part of our theory is built on his report of that interview. And he's careful. He had *Akers* watched. Three different visitors to *Akers* are known criminals."

"Have they seen Alderney?"

"I haven't been able to find out," said Trivett, "except in one case. A man named Link applied for a job. He's had three interviews, and Alderney hasn't made up his mind yet—according to reports. If Alderney is in touch with any of the thieves, interviewing them as applicants for work would be a pretty good way of seeing them, wouldn't it?"

Dawlish nodded. "Is there anything else?"

"That's the lot."

"It's slim enough," mused Dawlish aloud, "but I can see why you've marked him down. What do you want me to do?"

"You're as good a judge of a man as anyone," Trivett said, "and if you could scrape an acquaintance you might be able to pick up a little that will help us. There isn't any point in telling you what to do. You know what we're looking for, and you can judge an opportunity on the spot. And you've common cause."

Dawlish raised his eyebrows.

"In what?"

"You know what you're talking about when the subject is jewels," said Trivett. "Alderney doesn't hide the fact that he's a collector. In fact he's inclined to talk too much about it. He's conscious of his wealth and the power it gives him."

"What about his wife?" asked Dawlish.

Trivett said: "I don't know what to make of her. You say that Felicity likes her?"

"Yes—up to a point."

"What point?"

"If I read Felicity aright, she isn't too sure of the motives behind her charity work," said Dawlish. "She likes her; she even thinks a lot of her; but she suspects a hint of doing good for ulterior purposes—keeping up position, doing what her husband thinks she ought to do, and so on. Follow me?"

"Certainly I do," said Trivett. "I would expect Felicity to dislike her on that score."

"I haven't gone into it deeply with Fel," Dawlish admitted.

"Will you?"

"It looks as if I shall have to," said Dawlish, a little ruefully. "Is there anything else?"

"There's one other curious thing about Alderney," said Trivett. "He often interviews young women at *Akers*—with his wife's knowledge—and also in London. He says he's looking for the perfect secretary. Why he sees so many, I don't know."

"Have you got his fingerprints?"

"Not so far. He's cagey," said Trivett, "the kind of man who never slips up."

Outside the big hotel there were a dozen cars, all depositing their passengers. Trivett parked his own with some difficulty, and walked with Dawlish towards the big building. Tim Jeremy and Ted Beresford were waiting with the girls. The music from the band in the ballroom came to them clearly, and Anne Grayson was humming the melody beneath her breath.

"We'll be back in three minutes," Felicity said, and took her party off to the cloakroom. Dawlish looked about him, seeing several plainclothes men, two of whom he recognised as from Haslemere. A tall, burly man came up to them, and Trivett said:

"Here's Leven." He shook hands, and introduced Dawlish to the local Inspector. "How are things?" he asked.

"It's early yet," Leven said gloomily. "Alderney's here, he and his wife were among the first to arrive." He gave Dawlish the impression that there was something on his mind, and made it more than an impression as he went on: "Rummy and Flash Ben are in town," he added. "They haven't been near the hall yet, but it's not easy to check everyone in a crowd like this."

"Rummy and Flash Ben," echoed Dawlish.

Trivett said slowly: "Clever cracksmen, both of them. Rummy was one of Alderney's callers. I'm afraid that means trouble."

Chapter 3

PLEASURE

"What do you think of Anne?" inquired Dawlish.

"I didn't think Tim would make a fool of himself," said Felicity. "I'm delighted to see he hasn't."

"She's a nice child," agreed Dawlish.

"What about—"

A couple dancing too near banged into them, and the man apologised. Dawlish swung Felicity round in a quickstep, finding it easy to match her enjoyment. Like the dinner, the ball had gone without a single hitch. It was now half-past twelve. There had been no alarm, nothing to suggest that anything was amiss. Once, when the lights had flickered, Dawlish had been on edge lest this was a precursor to a raid; but they had quickly steadied again.

If jewel thieves were watching the ballroom, their eyes would be glistening. Alderney's wife had set the example; more jewels were gathered under this roof than had been seen for years. It was an open invitation to plunder, Dawlish commented to Trivett; and Trivett had agreed, worriedly. Alderney was dancing with his wife; he had danced many duty dances but not with any of

Dawlish's party. He seemed to be thoroughly enjoying himself, and Dawlish watched him covertly as he drew nearer.

Fairly tall, well-built, with dark hair going grey at the temples, he was a striking figure, a handsome and impressive man. He danced well. He was nearly always smiling. Debutantes and dowagers all seemed to enjoy his company. If this were a case of a man doing his duty, Alderney certainly seemed to be carrying it off with an air.

Lady Alderney recognised Felicity, and smiled.

Alderney glanced at Felicity, and immediately whispered something to his wife.

"If you weren't here—" began Dawlish.

"Be serious!"

"I am being serious. If you weren't here, she would be the loveliest woman in the room."

After a few steps, Felicity said: "I think I married you, darling, because you're such a beautiful liar."

They were near their table when the music stopped, and were sitting alone when Alderney and his wife came up. Dawlish rose quickly, Lady Alderney introduced her husband, and in a moment they were sitting at the table and Alderney was making himself extremely pleasant. At close quarters, Dawlish liked him; the man was something of a poseur, but, Dawlish thought, he had charm too, and a natural capacity for enjoyment.

The band struck up again, and Alderney smiled at Felicity.

"May I have this one?"

"May I?" Dawlish asked Lady Alderney.

She could dance well.

She looked into his eyes as he swept her round. Her own were large, grey, and rather sleepy; her lips were full. Dawlish thought 'sensuous' and dismissed the word, as being inappropriate in describing her extreme attraction. She showed no desire to talk until Dawlish led her back to her table, but then touched easily and emphatically on the various undertakings of country life.

"But I haven't come across your name on our committees," she added seriously.

"Felicity does enough for us both," Dawlish murmured.

"She would like your moral support, I'm sure."

"Oh, she has it," Dawlish assured her. "I keep fairly busy, you know. And—" he smiled broadly—"I have an aggressive temperament. Felicity can handle people far better than I, and is never likely to cause offence."

"A very polite refusal to serve," murmured Lady Alderney.

"Was it an invitation?" asked Dawlish, and then Alderney and Felicity came up, and another couple claimed their attention. The Dawlish's sauntered back to their table. Finding it deserted, they went into the buffet.

The *Four Ways* party was sitting happily chatting together. Trivett jumped up as they approached, but Tim got his word in first.

"Quick work, Pat!"

"They made the advance," Dawlish said. "Any news, Bill?"

"Oh, nothing will happen tonight," said Trivett. "How did you get on?"

"A modest triumph, I think."

Felicity looked from him to Trivett.

"What *is* this?"

Neither said anything.

"Grace, dear," said Felicity, sweetly, "if your thick-skulled husband has been talking to Pat about—"

"Shoes and ships and sealing wax," his glance flicking behind Felicity, in warning that people were within earshot. She held her peace, but, as they went back to the ballroom, insisted that he should drive her home. So it was arranged. The Trivetts, who were staying with Grace's people in Guildford, were to drive straight back, the others were spending two days at *Four Ways.*

The Alderneys came over to say *au revoir*, and Lady Alderney added:

"I haven't given up hope of persuading your husband to join our committees, Mrs. Dawlish."

"I won't be responsible for the trouble which might follow if you succeed," laughed Felicity darkly.

It was half-past one before they left the ballroom, and nearly two o'clock before they were in the cars. Tim was driving the others home, and had got off to a good start. A stream of cars was leaving Haslemere. In spite of Rummy and Flash Ben, reflected Dawlish, there had been no trouble.

"And now that I've got you alone," said Felicity "*what were all those nods and winks about?*"

"One wink and only half a nod," said Dawlish. "You do exaggerate so. The fact is, that there is slim, but trustworthy evidence that Alderney is not what he seems. Bill wants me to cultivate him."

After a long silence, Felicity said: "Alderney was most pressing that we should dine with them on Sunday."

"Was he indeed," murmured Dawlish.

"I don't like it."

"I can't say I do," admitted Dawlish. He fell silent, concentrating on his driving. Not far ahead, at the foot of the hill which led to Alum village, there were several cars with headlights shining close together. "It looks like a jam," he reflected, "I hope no one's had a spill. Too many people had too much to drink tonight."

"Including Tim," said Felicity.

"Oh, he can take it," Dawlish assured her. He was driving between thickets which hid the glow of headlights. Beyond they had to take a sharp turn. As they did so figures loomed suddenly out of the darkness.

Before he realised what was happening, a man stood squarely in front of the car, levelling an automatic. Dawlish jammed on the brakes. Other figures appeared out of the darkness. The speed and precision of the attack was bewildering.

"Get out, lady," said one of the men civilly enough.

Felicity sat rigid.

"Out, I said." the man repeated, and another appeared and opened Felicity's door. He also held a gun.

"What's this?" asked Dawlish, levelly.

"They call it a hold-up," said the man nearest him. "We won't hurt you, we only want the lady's jewels."

"Carry on, Fel," said Dawlish.

He knew the explanation of the grouped headlights, now; this was not the first hold-up. Another car was coming behind him, he could see the headlights swaying up and down, not a quarter of a mile away. He glanced at Felicity. The thief had taken off her brooch and a single string of pearls. Now he was holding her left hand, telling her to keep her wedding ring, and get back into the car. In the glow of headlights facing them, Felicity looked pale and stiff. The order came sharply to Dawlish. "Drive straight on and don't try any tricks, then you won't get hurt. I'm riding with you." He waved to the man who was still standing in front of the car, and the man moved, hurrying past Dawlish towards a position in which to stop the next car.

"*Don't do anything!*" Felicity muttered urgently.

Dawlish shook his head.

He let in the clutch and the car started off. He could have stretched out his hand and knocked the man out, but resisted the temptation. There were men lurking in the hedges, and he thought it likely that they were armed.

Not far ahead was the turning to *Four Ways* and Alum Village. Now Dawlish could see half a dozen cars parked along the narrow road, and he guessed that Beresford and Jeremy were waiting, cursing their helplessness just as he was cursing his.

"Pull in on the left," the man ordered, a moment later.

Dawlish obeyed. Felicity swayed towards him as he pulled in rather sharply.

"Sit tight," he whispered.

"Pat—"

Dawlish brought the car to a standstill, and put his hand on the handle of the door.

"Stay where you are," snapped the man. He stepped off, and Dawlish pushed the door sharply, thrusting it against him. Taken by surprise, the man staggered forward. He shouted as he fell, but Dawlish slipped out of the car before he could recover, and grabbed at his right hand. He touched the gun. The man tried to snatch his hand away, and others came hurrying, but Dawlish twisted his wrist until his grip relaxed.

Seizing the gun in his left hand Dawlish swung a wild blow at the other. He missed. Felicity flung her handbag at the man, who was about to bring the butt of a gun on Dawlish's forehead. It struck the man in the face, and made him miss by inches.

"*Action, there!*" roared Dawlish.

He met the rush of another attack head on. Obviously the thieves did not want to use their guns, that gave him a chance. He heard an answering shout, probably from Tim or Ted. A car engine started loudly. Another added to the sudden noise.

"Drive off!" Dawlish snapped to Felicity.

He jumped for the hedge as the string of cars began to move. There was still no shooting, but there was danger that one of these men might lose his head; a single shot could lead to an ugly business. Had he been right to act? He reached the cover of the hedge, hearing the heavy breathing of the men near him. He saw one, a dim figure in the dark, pointing a gun towards Felicity. He jumped forward, spoiling the man's aim. As he did so, a tremendous shout went up:

"*Tally-hoooo!*"

Only one man in the world had such a voice as that: Ted Beresford. In the faint light from the headlights, now rapidly disappearing, he saw Beresford, Tim and half a dozen other men rushing towards him. The men who had turned to attack turned again, to fly. Dawlish threw caution to the winds and chased after them. There was a chance that the men with the jewels would be taken by surprise, and be caught. Their car, he reasoned, was further along the road. At the first alarm, they would rush towards it; presumably their first thought would be to get away with the jewels they had already collected.

Tim caught up with him.

"Which way?"

"Over that hedge," said Dawlish. "No—there's a gate just here."

Ten yards further along they came upon the gate, just visible against the sky. Dawlish vaulted it easily, Tim came down badly and slipped. Dawlish waited for him.

"If we can get to the corner we might stop 'em," he said. "We'll have to take a chance."

As they ran, they heard a car engine. Side-lights were just visible through the hedge.

"We'll make it," gasped Jeremy.

The cars started off as they reached the opposite hedge, and was almost level with them. Dawlish drew a deep breath, steadied himself, and levelled the gun. He could only hope to hit one of the rear wheels; if the tyre did blow out, they would have a chance of regaining the booty; it seemed a slim chance, but it was worth taking.

Dawlish fired four times.

The sharp reports hummed loudly on the still night air.

"I've missed," thought Dawlish. Suddenly there was an explosion, and the car slewed round.

"Got 'em!" exclaimed Tim, exultantly.

"Careful now," said Dawlish. "They'll be nasty."

They scrambled through the hedge, and could just see the driver of the car getting out; he had a bag in one hand and a gun in the other. He raised the gun and pointed, firing at point-blank range. Dawlish flung himself to one side. Jeremy went on, and Dawlish heard the two men collide. Footsteps sounded loud on the roadway now, and it seemed more likely to Dawlish that they were the thieves collaborators rather than his own.

He got up, his head whirling. Tim and a man were struggling near the car. A flash, pointing towards the sky, came almost simultaneously with the report of the shot. Tim was holding one of the man's arms upwards, while the other clutched the case.

Dawlish pulled at it.

The man held on, but was unable to concentrate on holding his gun.

"Got it!" cried Tim.

Dawlish tugged the case away, and flung it towards the hedge. Tim got a stranglehold on his opponent, but the approaching footsteps were dangerously near. Dawlish went forward, picked the man up bodily, and flung him over the hedge. The man lodged on top for a moment, and then slid out of sight. Dawlish grabbed Tim's arm.

"Keep back," he said.

The rest of the hold-up men, having reached their car, found that the rear tyre was punctured. They went running off, some along the road, some across the fields, while a stream of angry men in evening dress followed them. Beresford limped in the rear of this cavalcade, and stopped when Dawlish called him.

They were all together when Dawlish opened the case. Inside were the jewels.

"That was a lot of trouble for nothing," Beresford said in a satisfied voice.

Dawlish smiled. "I wonder. There may have been hold-ups on the other roads, you know."

There had been four hold-ups, two of them larger in scale than that on the Godalming Road. The other three had been completely successful; it was too early yet to assess the value of the stolen jewels. The story was gradually built up after an interview with Inspector Leven. Trivett, Leven thought, had been allowed to go through; he had been one of the first to drive along the Guildford road.

"You got some of the beggars, didn't you?" asked Dawlish.

"Three," said Leven, "as well as the one you threw over the hedge, and I think he's probably the only one who matters."

"Have you seen him?"

"Only for a few minutes. He won't talk."

"What about the Alderneys?"

Leven sucked his lips in repressively.

"They were robbed."

"I didn't expect anything else," said Felicity, coming into the room with a tray of sandwiches and coffee. "Are you still *in camera*, may I ask?"

"There's nothing else confidential; as far as I know," said the Inspector, glumly. He accepted a cup of coffee, and then looked miserably at his toes. "The Chief Constable's wife had a necklace worth a fortune."

"People shouldn't have necklaces worth a fortune," declared

Anne Grayson, coming in. She laughed. "I can afford to be smug. Mine was paste."

"I nearly screamed when they took my engagement ring," Joan Beresford announced. She looked more tired than any of the others. "You have got it back, Pat, haven't you?"

"It'll be in the bag," Dawlish assured her. "Share-out tomorrow morning. And it's time we started getting ready for bed," he added. "No, don't hurry, Leven!"

Leven did hurry, nevertheless, and Dawlish and the others finished their coffee and went upstairs. They were still talking animatedly. Beresford and Tim had been caught in exactly the same way as Dawlish, and Tim had chosen to try an attack about the same time as Dawlish. Both men had been quick to realise that their only chance had been to submit without protestation, and then to spring a surprise.

Alone with Felicity, he mused:

"I feel sorry for Leven and Bill."

"Why?" asked Felicity, and added: "I mean, why sorrier for them than for the victims?"

Dawlish pulled off his singlet.

"Because, my sweet, they took all precautions at the ball-room, the place was thick with plainclothes men and the streets patrolled by flat-foots. Trivett was sure that something would be attempted tonight, but when the show was over, it looked as if the attempt had been frustrated by the imposing gallery of detectives. The hold-ups on the road weren't anticipated and—you're tired," he broke off, abruptly, "or you wouldn't want to be told."

"I'm tired out," Felicity murmured, and then added: "And worried."

"Your ring will be—"

"I'm not thinking about my ring," Felicity said, "I'm thinking about you. Pat."

"Hm-hm?"

"How many men did they use altogether?"

"A dozen or so," said Dawlish, lightly.

"Two dozen or so," corrected Felicity. "It's highly organised. They—they acted as coolly as traffic cops!"

Dawlish laughed. "Yes, they're pretty efficient."

"Pat," said Felicity, standing between the beds, "there were between twenty and thirty men, all told, which means an extremely good and powerful organisation. You have the damndest way of getting mixed up in this kind of thing."

"Well, we were warned," Dawlish said. "It would have happened to us whether Bill had been down here or not. And I suppose I would have acted in pretty well the same way."

Felicity turned down her bed, and then Dawlish's. "Are you really serious about suspecting the Alderneys?"

"Trivett is."

"With good reason?"

"Fairly good."

"In spite of the fact that they were robbed?"

"Of course," said Dawlish. "That doesn't make a tittle of difference. And in view of what happened tonight, I can't very well refuse Trivett's invitation to get to know the Alderneys better. After all," he reasoned, as Felicity slipped into bed, "if they're guilty, well and good, and if they're not we'll have made a couple of interesting acquaintances. I wish Alderney weren't such a likeable customer," he added, as he switched off the light and pulled back the curtains. "I quite took—"

He broke off, abruptly; for outside the window he saw the head and shoulders of a man.

Chapter 4

A PIECE OF ROPE

"Good-morning," said Dawlish dryly.

The man at the window neither moved nor spoke.

Dawlish was aware of a sense of unreality and an uncomfortable feeling that the man outside might, when he did decide to move, act quickly.

The window was open at the top, but not at the bottom. To get at the man, Dawlish would have to fling the window up or break the glass; neither could be done without giving the fellow ample opportunity to take action. Felicity's bed was in line with the window, and if it came to shooting, she might get hurt. These were the practical issues. The window was perhaps thirty feet above the ground, and if he broke the glass and at the same time sent the man toppling from the ladder on which he appeared to be standing, a neck might be broken; only live men tell tales.

There was an impressive quality about the organisation of this night's events. Here was a man, not simply listening, but standing there impassively, as if all he wanted to do was to unnerve Dawlish. It was essential that he should not be allowed to get away; for he had learned of the official suspicion of Alderney.

These things flashed through Dawlish's mind as Felicity sat up in bed and stared at him.

"All right," said Dawlish, and stealthily picked up a hairbrush from the dressing-table. "If you prefer it, good-evening."

"Pat," murmured Felicity.

Dawlish waved a hand behind him.

"Pat, are you—"

"*Hush!*" hissed Dawlish, and then went on in a louder voice: "I shouldn't stay there too long, if I were you."

A faint swish of bed covers told him Felicity was getting out.

"Keep away from the window," Dawlish whispered. There was a touch of fantasy about that too, for low-pitched though he kept his voice, it was impossible to prevent the man from hearing him.

Dawlish tightened his grip on the hairbrush.

Felicity had reached the wall.

"Get one of the others. Tell him to go outside."

Felicity slipped, as swiftly and as flatly as she could, through the door, for she was not unversed in the ways of violent criminals. Dawlish raised the brush, hoping to create a brief diversion. His bewilderment was increasing; it was not natural for a man to stand there so impassively, staring at him, unblinking—

Unblinking!

"Fel!" called Dawlish.

Felicity stopped by the door.

"Switch on the light, will you?" asked Dawlish.

Felicity hesitated, then obeyed. The man outside did not blink, although the main light over the dressing-table was shining into his eyes.

"What—what is it?" asked Felicity.

"Warn the others," said Dawlish in a strained voice, and glanced over his, shoulder. Only when Felicity had left the room did he push up the window. The man's head and shoulders swung round a little as Dawlish stretched out a hand and touched him.

This man was dead.

With the light shining on him, Dawlish examined the body more closely. A rope was tied about his shoulders and looped under his arms from above; that was why he had appeared to be standing on top of a ladder. Again Dawlish touched him, and again he swayed, as if moved by a gentle breeze.

A footstep sounded in the passage.

"What's the trouble?" called Beresford.

"Go downstairs with Tim, will you, and be careful," Dawlish said. "There may be one or two men about. I've got a deado here."

Beresford grunted, and went on his way; he acted automatically and with no show of surprise.

Felicity came back, and Dawlish could hear Anne Grayson's whispering voice. Dawlish, not wanting Felicity or Anne on the scene, sent them downstairs to telephone Trivett and the Haslemere police.

Beresford and Jeremy, in pyjamas and dressing-gowns, reached the side of the house, and looked up. Dawlish could see them clearly in the light from the drawing-room window, which Felicity had just switched on.

"What do you say you've got up there?" asked Tim.

"Just a corpse," Dawlish said. "Fetch a ladder, will you?"

He did not wait for the ladder to arrive, but hurried to the bathroom, removed the hatch-cover of the loft, and hauled himself into it. Here he opened the dormer window, which was immediately above his bedroom, and shone a torch about the roof. He saw the rope, tied about a stout nail which had been driven into the eaves. Crawling out of the window, he rested the torch on the ledge so that it gave him some light, and then approached the edge of the roof. He did not attempt to haul the body up until Tim had put a ladder into position. Then Tim held the weight of the body and Dawlish pulled. Soon, he dragged the dead man into the attic.

A quarter of an hour later, the body was lying on a couch in the boxroom, and the party gathered in the drawing-room. Anne looked excited rather than scared. Her hair was flying loose, her eyes were bright, and in a scarlet dressing-gown she looked a lovely little creature.

"What did Leven say?" Dawlish asked Felicity.

"That he'll be here soon," Felicity told him. "Bill wasn't home. Grace said she would tell him as soon as he arrived. He sent her on ahead of him, apparently. Pat, what happened to the man upstairs."

Dawlish looked at Anne.

"I'm hardened," Anne assured him, quickly.

Dawlish smiled. "That's as well. He was killed by a knife thrust in the back. Rigor is setting in fairly fast, which probably means that he's been dead two or three hours. A doctor might be able to make a better guess."

Anne exclaimed: "That means—" and then her voice trailed off.

"It means that he was hanging out there when we came home," Dawlish said, "and was probably killed while we were at the ball. A nice touch." He smiled mirthlessly.

"Why did they hang him here?" asked Felicity, her voice low.

"Your guess is as good as mine," said Dawlish, and then he heard the sound of a car. "Look here, Fel, go back to bed. You will be resting even if you don't get to sleep. So will you, Anne.

Go to our room," he added, "I'll nip in with Tim when Leven's gone."

He watched them as they went out of the room. Now that she knew the truth, Anne was more shocked than he had expected. Felicity too, was deeply troubled, fearful of how deeply he himself would become involved.

Beresford had gone to open the door to Leven.

He came in, his eyes red-rimmed and glassy.

"Well, what's the trouble?"

Dawlish told him in a few terse words, adding that Chloe had been out for the night, not wanting to be alone in the house until the early hours of the morning. Leven started when he heard about the body, but did not move from his chair. He heard Dawlish out, and then got up.

"I'd better have a look at him," he said. "Have you any idea who he is?"

"None at all."

"You haven't seen him before?"

"No."

"I suppose you know what this means," Leven asked, with a heavy frown.

"I can guess," said Dawlish, and led the way upstairs.

His guess was the same as Leven's, as Felicity's. Trivett's visit to *Four Ways* had been observed. The dead body had been hung from the roof in a macabre warning to the effect that interest in this affair would not be healthy. Such an act called for ruthlessness which, in spite of everything else, rather appealed to Dawlish. Now that the initial shock was over, he felt that he had the measure of the people whom Trivett was fighting. It was not surprising that the police were troubled and that the Home Office was pressing for results. It was not even surprising that in spite of a traditional dislike of consulting outsiders, the Assistant

Commissioner at Scotland Yard had agreed that Trivett should discuss the affair with Dawlish.

It was half-past four; an hour earlier, Dawlish had been tired out; but now his step was light and there was a gleam in his eyes which Tim and Ted knew of old.

They went quietly up the stairs, past the main bedrooms. Dawlish opened the door of the boxroom, and Leven stepped inside.

Immediately, he gave an exclamation of annoyance. "Might I ask one of you to telephone the police-surgeon, Haslemere 3645? I ought to have thought of it before." The testy tone of his voice showed that he was annoyed with himself because, being so tired, he had forgotten an elementary thing. Photographers and finger-print men would be wanted, too, he added, as Tim went out of the door.

"I'll have a word with the police station," Tim promised, and then Leven stepped forward and lifted the sheet from the dead man's head.

The face was unmarked; a sallow face, with a prominent nose, the eyes set wide apart. Dark hair grew far back on the forehead. The whole was etched clearly in Dawlish's eyes.

Then he realised that Leven was standing quite still.

He felt a tremor of excitement. "Do you know him?"

Leven said heavily: "Yes, I know him all right It's FlashBen."

Beresford exclaimed: "One of the men you were talking about tonight, by George!"

"I thought he would have a crack at the ballroom," Leven said in a level voice. "Things certainly haven't gone according to expectations."

"It looks as if thieves have fallen out," murmured Dawlish. An almost happy lilt ran through his voice. "You've a lot to do, Leven!"

"Yes, haven't we?" amended Beresford, dryly.

Before long, the police-surgeon and the police arrived, and the roof was alive with crawling figures. It had been warm, early in the evening, and the prints of the men who had put Flash Ben up there would be clear from their moist finger-tips—if they had been careless enough to disregard the wearing of gloves. Dawlish did not think there was much likelihood of carelessness in this particular business. Trivett telephoned his decision to leave the immediate investigation to Leven. Two men were stationed in the grounds of the house, a precautionary measure that Dawlish thought unnecessary, but for which he was nevertheless grateful on the girls' account.

Making his way to the spare room Dawlish was asleep within five minutes of his head touching the pillow.

He did not dream.

It was late when he woke up.

He lay for a few minutes in drowsy content until his mind, comfortably blank, registered the fact that he was too hot, and he pushed back the blankets. Then he looked at the window and saw that the sun was high. At once he remembered what had happened the night before. He glanced at his watch; it was half-past eleven.

He got up and went to the window; the little spare room looked over the front garden, the colourful flower-beds and the trim lawns. Benson, a young gardener and general factotum who lived in the village, was trimming a privet hedge which separated the flower and vegetable gardens.

By the gate stood a policeman.

Dawlish smiled grimly and made his way to the bathroom. He heard Beresford's deep voice coming from the dining-room. Felicity said something lightly and Joan laughed. That was a good sign; Dawlish had been genuinely worried about Felicity's reaction to the trouble. He finished bathing and shaving at speed and ran downstairs to join them.

He patted Anne's shoulder, Joan's arm, and Felicity's head; and then he dropped a kiss on her forehead. "Could there be a cup of tea?"

Felicity was already pouring one out.

"Well, what wild theories have you been evolving in my absence?"

"We're all going on a long, blissful holiday," said Felicity.

"That'll be fine," said Dawlish, "but the apples have got to be picked first."

"Too true, dear boy. But will such a simple, innocent ploy content you now, after last night's challenge to your vanity?"

"Vanity!" echoed Dawlish. "Darling, it was an insult."

"Ted says that the dead man was a crook," contributed Joan, soberly.

"A known crook," complemented Dawlish. "There are two varieties—known and unknown." He sipped his tea, and watched Felicity. She appeared not to be greatly upset by what had happened. Dawlish smiled to himself; he was always imagining that Felicity would make difficulties, whereas in fact she had never made a serious one yet. It was more or less compulsory to help the police now; there would be no argument, a man hanging from his own roof having given him a close personal interest.

Beresford murmured: "You're bright this morning, aren't you?"

"My dear chap, who wouldn't be in this company?" Dawlish passed his cup to be refilled, and glanced out of the window. As he did so, a car turned into the drive; it was half-way to the house before the others heard it.

"Who's that?" asked Felicity quickly.

"One large, powerful car with silent engine," murmured Dawlish. "I shouldn't be enormously surprised if it turned out to be Alderney."

Chapter 5

SIR BRIAN ALDERNEY

They were all looking towards the door, when Chloe came in. If she knew why the policemen were in the grounds, she showed no signs of being flustered. Now, she smiled.

"Sir Brian Alderney has called, ma'am, to see Mr. Dawlish."

Dawlish pushed his chair back.

"Oh, all right," said Felicity, resignedly.

"Can anyone recommend a good, draught-proof spot for eavesdropping?" asked Ted, in a loud whisper.

"Don't be an oaf!" exclaimed Joan.

"I'll report in due course," Dawlish promised, and went out, tightening the sash-cord of his dressing-gown.

Alderney was standing by the window, and turned immediately. If he were startled to find Dawlish so informally dressed, he hid it well. He stepped forward with his hand outstretched, and as Dawlish took it, he summed him up afresh in the light of day. Undoubtedly he was a good-looking man. His smile was friendly, he was well turned out, wearing a light tweed suit and a quiet tie.

"Shouldn't it be Major Dawlish?" he asked.

Dawlish smiled.

"Officially, yes."

"But you prefer to be—*incognito?*" Alderney paused slightly before the word

"Have it that way if you like," said Dawlish. "Sit down, won't you?" He offered cigarettes and pulled up a chair. "Is it too early for a drink?"

"I don't drink before the evening," said Alderney.

"Good practise," murmured Dawlish.

"It's one way of keeping awake after luncheon," said Alderney, and smiled again. "I have to congratulate you."

"Oh?" murmured Dawlish.

"On your remarkable effort last night," said Alderney warmly. "I only wish I had been on the same road, my wife might not then be grieving for her lost jewels."

"Oh, that," said Dawlish. "The mugs gave me a chance and I took it. I do hope Lady Alderney hasn't suffered too heavily."

"Far too heavily," said Alderney, lightly enough.

"I *am* sorry," Dawlish said, and sounded sincere.

Alderney shrugged.

"She was one of many, but I've no doubt that you know that the hold-ups on the other roads were successful. I hope that the police will quickly recover the jewels, but—" he shrugged again, and his eyes narrowed slightly.

"Have you much confidence in the police, Mr. Dawlish?"

"They do a good job on the whole," Dawlish said.

"I wonder," murmured Alderney.

"That sounds almost cynical," said Dawlish.

"I suppose it does," agreed Alderney, as he crossed his legs.

Dawlish was trying to work out what lay behind this visit and this deliberate turn in the conversation, but he gave no sign beyond a polite interest.

"I don't think the police showed very much imagination last night, do you?" Alderney went on.

"Perhaps it bourgeoned in the wrong direction," laughed Dawlish. "They made a guess, and it turned out wrong."

"Could they really have suspected that the ballroom would be raided?" asked Alderney. "It seems so unlikely that even the most daring of thieves would attempt to raid such a gathering at such a time. And there were so many police about that one would have thought any such plan would have been scotched from the outset."

"Yes," said Dawlish. "But I don't really think we can blame the police for not thinking of the road hold-ups, you know. Did *you* think of it?"

Alderney looked blank.

"I had no reason to suspect trouble of any kind. Had you?"

Dawlish smiled. If Alderney knew the truth and Trivett's suspicions were well-founded, he knew of the body outside the window; by the same token, he suspected the reason for Trivett's call here on the previous night.

If he were quite innocent, it did not matter what he knew.

"Yes," said Dawlish, "I had."

Alderney's eyebrows shot up. "Did you, by Jove!"

"Superintendent Trivett of New Scotland Yard is a friend of mine," Dawlish said, lightly, "and he was with our party last evening. He told me that the local police were on the alert, because of several jewel robberies in the district. So I was half-prepared—but I didn't expect the road hold-ups."

"Yet you have had a lot of experience in this sort of thing, haven't you?" asked Alderney.

Dawlish laughed. "Who's been talking?"

"My dear Dawlish, the whole district knows your reputation," Alderney said. "No, I'm not joking. There was that spectacular affair in which a chap called Bland was involved. I remember it quite well."

"Yes?" said Dawlish.

Alderney leaned back in his chair.

"I knew Algernon L. Bland," he informed Dawlish, "and I've never met a more likeable rogue! He *was* a rogue, but he had his points—even you'll admit that."

"Oh, yes," said Dawlish. "A modern brigand."

"You've got it exactly," Alderney said, with some enthusiasm. "I always suspected the truth about him, but I was almost sorry when you caught him." He laughed.

Dawlish looked blank.

"And you would be surprised how eagerly some of the local people read up your cases and learned just what you'd done," went on the visitor. "It isn't really surprising that after last night's events *and* after learning that you had managed to recapture the jewels stolen on this road, they decided to appeal to you for help, is it?"

"Appeal to *me*," said Dawlish, faintly.

"That's why I'm here," said Alderney. "I saved you from receiving a deputation of half a dozen. The recent robberies and the failure of the police to catch the men or recover the lost property have weakened faith in the police. With a giant of detection among them, like you, it's logical that the local residents should invite your help. I wouldn't be in your shoes," added Alderney with a chuckle. "They will expect miracles!"

"I ought to feel flattered," murmured Dawlish.

Alderney leaned forward.

"Seriously, I do hope you'll accept."

"But seriously, how can I?" laughed Dawlish, shortly, "accept such an invitation to knight errantry? If I can help the police, as a law-abiding citizen I cannot very well refuse, but—"

"That's something gained," said Alderney.

"Who are the ring-leaders in this appeal to an amateur sleuth?" asked Dawlish, allowing to appear a little frown of petulance.

"The last people you'd expect. Colonel Maitland, Lady Fripp, the Courtlands—and oh, of course, it's understood that you'll have all expenses met," Alderney went on. Dawlish could not help thinking that there was a measure of mockery in those grey eyes. "There'll be a general fund, and—"

"What nonsense is this!" exclaimed Dawlish. "Surely you don't expect me to take you seriously. I'm not usually a fiery bloke but I consider your mission goes beyond the bounds of what is permissible."

"Now, Dawlish—"

Dawlish leapt to his feet. "The police fail on one or two little jobs, a few people lose their baubles, and they send you with this—" he broke off, pettishly. "Have they forgotten that I grow apples?" he demanded.

"Apples?" echoed Alderney.

"Certainly, apples. I work for my living. I have not come here to retire. I'm fruit-farming, I'm busy and—"

"I'm sorry you've taken it like this," said Alderney. "I hoped you would agree to help. It is more serious than you think, you know." He offered cigarettes, and seemed relieved when Dawlish accepted one. He flicked a lighter, and Dawlish muttered, "Thanks."

"Look here, Dawlish," went on Alderney, "I can tell you that the insurance companies are worried by the police failure, and I'm told that the Home Office is taking it very seriously. It's not a case of the thieves getting away with one or two trifling robberies. Last night's affair surely convinced you of that. It's very well organised and—well, in my opinion your direct methods are more likely to get quick results than anything the police can do."

"The police can be direct."

Alderney stood up, looked at him with an eyebrow raised, and then asked unexpectedly:

"Did you get any sleep at all last night?"

"What on earth made you ask that?"

"You don't seem yourself," said Alderney. "I can't think you would wilfully misunderstand me. After all, Dawlish, but for your own good fortune, your wife and friends would have suffered just as badly as anyone else. No one seriously expects you to work miracles, but in view of your experience, you might reasonably be expected to help."

"It is a view," Dawlish said, "though not necessarily mine."

"I still hope that it might be," said Alderney. He gave a set smile and moved towards the door. "Telephone me if you change your mind."

"I will," promised Dawlish.

When the Rolls Royce moved down the drive, the little party in the dining-room were looking out of the window. Dawlish went in, without them seeing him.

"Did they quarrel?" Tim was asking.

"It takes a lot to make Pat lose his temper," observed Felicity, and then saw him standing in the doorway.

Dawlish grinned.

"Thank you for those kind words," he said. "I wanted to see if Alderney would jump—he jumped all right!" He chuckled. "I've a feeling that Alderney got a lot that he didn't bargain for."

Felicity was frowning.

"Was there any need to bellow at him?"

"He isn't likely to welcome you in future," observed Anne.

"Closed door at *Akers*," murmured Joan.

"It will be wide open the moment I step on the porch," said

Dawlish, confidently. "Alderney may be our villain, and it doesn't do for the villain of the piece to feel too confident or think he knows exactly how to handle all concerned. Just now he's telling himself that I'm a conceited buffoon—"

"Here, here!" murmured Tim.

"And trying to make up his mind how much of what I said was serious," Dawlish declared, ignoring the interruption. "Let him ponder for an hour or two." He glanced at Felicity. "Are you in a betting mood?" he asked.

"No," answered Felicity.

"That's a pity," said Dawlish. "I was going to bet you a bushel of pippins to a new pipe that before the day's out Lady Alderney or one of her cronies will be asking you to use your influence with me."

"I wonder," said Felicity, doubtfully.

"Why should they want you so badly?" asked Anne.

Dawlish beamed as the door opened and Chloe came in with a laden tray.

"They probably don't. A's put them up to it—thanks, Chloe, you're a treasure." He waited until she had gone out, and then added: "If Alderney's our man, what neater move could there be than getting me to work with him? That way he'd be a jump ahead every time. Want a job, Tim?"

"Yes," said Tim, promptly.

"Jobs go by seniority," declared Beresford.

"There's more than enough for two," said Dawlish. "Put on your best bibs and tuckers, and make a few calls. Mr. Dawlish asked you to have a word with them, and—"

"With whom?"

"Colonel Maitland, Lady Fripp, the Courtlands and one or two other local blockbusters," said Dawlish. "Do they seriously want me to help? The object of all these intense inquiries being," he added, "to find out whether Alderney first put the idea into their heads."

"I see," said Felicity, slowly.

Dawlish winked at Anne.

"You can hunt in pairs," he said. "Good riding!"

At half-past one Trivett telephoned. Dawlish advised him to stay away from *Four Ways* for the time being. Despite the continued presence of policemen, Dawlish thought that the house was being watched by the thieves, and he did not want it known that he was in close touch with Scotland Yard. Trivett agreed, and went over the incidents of the night before; there were no real clues as to the murder of Flash Ben, except that he had almost certainly been killed in a field near Alum Village, where the police had discovered grim signs of a struggle.

There were no prints in the house.

The men who had planted the body had obviously known that the house would be deserted for a specific time.

Dawlish did not tell Trivett about Alderney's offer; he wanted more information about that before he talked too freely.

At a quarter to three, when Dawlish was busying himself in the orchard, dressed in his old Norfolk jacket and corduroys, a Daimler came along the drive. Three quarters of an hour later, Felicity hurried across the rough grass to where she saw Dawlish atop a ladder placed against the branches of a heavily laden Bramley tree.

"Hi there!"

"Hallo?"

"You've won!"

Dawlish pushed the branches aside, to look down on her excited face.

"Won what?"

"The bet you didn't make. Lady Alderney wants me to use my influence to make you accept her husband's suggestion!"

Tim Jeremy and Anne Grayson turned into the drive of *Four Ways* a little after six o'clock, smiling at each other. As a result, Tim scraped the nearside wing against the bank. This incident Dawlish saw from his bedroom window. As the car drew up he called out:

"That'll cost you thirty bob. Damage to the drive."

"Never mind your perishing drive, look at my wing," yelled Tim, fingering the wing fondly. "The drive's a yard too narrow, it's a public danger." He grinned. "We'll be seeing you!" He took Anne's arm, and they disappeared into the house.

Dawlish came hurrying downstairs.

"Before you all start talking, you'll want some tea," said Felicity. "I'll get—"

"Tea!" exclaimed Anne. "No, *please!*"

"Tea," groaned Tim. "I'm aswim with it. Cakes galore and three lots of cream—" He closed his eyes.

Dawlish looked at them with his head on one side.

"Yes, we understand that you've had a good meal."

"Seven," said Anne.

"Starting at three-fifteen and finishing at five-thirty," Tim declared. "Non-stop."

"They're so sure that Mr. Dawlish—but shouldn't it be Major?—would solve the problem," murmured Anne.

"Such a big, handsome man," added Tim.

"So quick-witted."

"So courageous."

"So direct!"

"Sir Brian Alderney is *never* wrong," intoned Tim. "The

moment he suggested it, they jumped at the suggestion. They had not yet heard from him, about the interview he had promised to have with Mr. Dawlish, and they were delighted that Mr.—but shouldn't it be Major?—Dawlish was taking some interest in the affair. They were not to be misunderstood. They knew Major-Mister would do the work out of the gooodness of his heart, but it wasn't fair that he should be expected to meet the out of pocket expenses."

"Congratulate us."

"Congratulations," said Dawlish, absently. "So he did put them up to it. I—hallo, here come the others."

Ted and Joan had encountered the same enthusiasm, and much the same hospitality.

Felicity, glancing at Dawlish, judged from his expression that he did not want to indulge in idle chatter just then and, on some pretext, took the two women out of the room. Tim helped himself to a tankard of beer, and sat astride a chair. Beresford stuck his artificial leg on a pouffe, and smiled faintly.

"It gets tired," he said.

"What's making you so quiet, Patrick?" asked Tim.

Dawlish raised an eyebrow.

"I'm puzzled."

"Everything seems obvious enough to me," said Tim. "These people have been stung, and they're reacting against the police who, in their conceit, they think should have given them foolproof service. None of them is really worth a string of beans." The beer seemed to have sobered Tim. "I can't honestly say that I had any liking for any of them—with the possible exception of Lady Fripp, who has a wicked eye. But she's obsessed by the loss of a diamond heirloom. What did you make of your bunch, Ted?"

Beresford hesitated before he replied.

"Much the same on the surface. But the people are all right. Limited vision in some cases, and they do feel annoyed—who wouldn't? Underneath it all, I would say that they're scared."

Tim looked puzzled.

"About a repetition, do you mean?"

"Could be. Incidentally, they eat out of Alderney's hand."

"There you have it," said Dawlish, and the others looked at him in some surprise, for there was much emphasis in his words.

Neither of the others spoke.

"They're all eating out of Alderney's hand," Dawlish repeated. "The fellow's been here for three years, that's only a year more than we have, and he's already king of the castle. He drops a hint, and they seize upon it and magnify it. They want me to help, simply and solely because they're convinced that Alderney's right, because he inspired the idea, and so—*he* really wants me to join up with him. Thus, everything I do will be an open book to him, and he can make his own plans accordingly. Right?"

Tim frowned.

"You're rather taking it for granted that he is the Big Bad Wolf, aren't you?"

"I'm going to be very surprised if he isn't," said Dawlish.

It would have been difficult to explain even to his friends why he felt so sure that Alderney was not what he seemed. It was not because of the evidence which Trivett had given him, although without that he doubted whether he would have formed the opinion. It was not wholly the result of their interview that morning, or of the discoveries which had been made during the afternoon. The key, thought Dawlish, was in Alderney's bland smile when he had talked of a 'likeable rogue', and the hint of mockery in Alderney's eyes.

Judging from what he knew so far, Alderney was another likeable rogue.

The other two agreed with him. They always had. It seemed to all three, however, that Alderney was going to be a difficult man to bring to book.

Tim said at last: "Let's face it, there isn't any real evidence at all, Pat. Where are you going to start?"

"We could have a look round *Akers*," Dawlish said, mildly.

"You mean—break in?" demanded Tim.

Dawlish grinned.

"Not for a start. The next step is obviously one from me. I'll go over to *Akers* this evening. I wonder if Alderney knows that the police are watching his house?" he added. "I'll have a word with Leven first, I think."

Leven was able to give him the information he wanted. The big house was watched from three points of vantage, the watchers with binoculars and powerful cameras. A record of Alderney's visitors was carefully taken; the results, Dawlish already knew.

Dawlish took his car out, a little after eight o'clock, and without telephoning to say that he was coming, drove to *Akers*. The grounds were extensive, and Dawlish was nearing a small lodge as he breasted the crown of a hill. This would be one of the police crow's nests, he thought idly, and glanced towards a thicket in which half a dozen men could easily be hidden.

He saw no one, but he did see an odd thing. A trilby hat was hanging on a high branch of a beech tree. The hat waved gently in the breeze, and Dawlish slowed down and sat for some minutes, looking at it.

Chapter 6

THE HAT WITHOUT A MAN

By the side of the road was a heap of flints. Dawlish got out of the car and strolled towards it. Picking up one of a suitable size he shied it vigorously. The flint soared half a yard to the left of the hat. He tried again, with even less success.

The third time he was luckier. The hat toppled, seemed about to fall, and then stopped.

Determined now to bring the hat down, he aimed a rapid fusillade of flints. Down fell the trilby, to lodge on a branch which Dawlish could reach with ease.

Satisfied, Dawlish stretched up a vigorous arm. As he did so, a voice came from behind him.

"Well aimed, sir."

It was a mild, congratulatory voice with a curious timbre; he was not at first sure whether it was a man's or a woman's. It had a note of culture and one of mild surprise; altogether it intrigued Dawlish but, as was his way, he did not turn round immediately, but examined the hat. It was nearly new, and inside was the tag of a Haslemere shopkeeper. He tried it on; it was much too small.

"Unbecoming," the voice again.

"I was afraid it would be," said Dawlish, and turned with a smile. The man standing near him almost sent the smile from his face. He was dressed in garments which had long passed the chance of being described as shabby. He was carrying a canvas bag, startlingly new. On his feet were once-white tennis shoes, frayed at the toe.

Dawlish watched him narrowly. The voice was all wrong; the man's manner was all wrong. He had met tramps of all sizes and descriptions, but none with the air of culture which sounded in this man's voice.

"I am told," said the tramp, "that hats have become very expensive to buy."

"So I understand," agreed Dawlish. "I don't often wear them, so—"

"You were hoping it would fit a friend of yours, perhaps?"

"Not exactly," said Dawlish.

The tramp smiled. "In that case, I, myself, could do with a new hat."

Dawlish glanced at his battered headgear. There was mystery about this man, for in addition to his cultured voice, he had good teeth, an uncommon feature among tramps.

"Have you considered, sir, the oddness of this situation? It is not unusual to find a man without a hat. It is, however, unusual to find a hat without a man."

"Undoubtedly," said Dawlish.

"And there was a man here not long ago," said the tramp.

"Are you sure?"

"Perfectly sure. I passed the time of day with him. He was a little curt." The smile flashed again, and Dawlish thought of Alderney's phrase—'a likeable rogue'. But was there any evidence that this man was a rogue?

"Was he wearing a hat?" asked Dawlish.

"Yes. That hat."

"How can you identify it?" asked Dawlish.

"By the white patch on the side," said the tramp dreamily. "He was annoyed by the white patch, sir. He was uncomplimentary towards the habits of birds on the wing."

"Oh," said Dawlish. "Where have you been since you saw him?"

"To Alderney House," said the tramp.

It was on the tip of Dawlish's tongue to say: "You mean *Akers*," but he saved himself. He was satisfied that the tramp was not all that he appeared to be; for would a tramp know that the name of the owner of the house was Alderney? Wasn't it a mistake more likely to be made by a man who knew who lived there and was not just passing by?

"How were you received?" asked Dawlish gravely.

"With fair courtesy," said the tramp, and touched the bag. "I was fortunate enough to secure this, but not, as I had hoped, to find a few days' work and perhaps to enjoy the privilege of sleeping in a comfortable barn. It has been a good summer, but I have little liking for sleeping under the hedges. The dew gathers surprisingly thick in these late summer nights. But I was given a meal, for which I was grateful, and a two shilling piece."

"And the bag?"

"And the bag."

"Then you certainly shouldn't grumble," said Dawlish, "but if you really want to sleep in a shed or barn—"

"I do!"

"And you want a few days' work?"

"Most assuredly!"

"Sawing logs?"

"It would be inaccurate for me to pretend that I am an expert at sawing logs," said the little man, judicially, "but on the other hand, I know which end of the saw to hold. Can you recommend such a place to me?"

"Call at *Four Ways* a little after nine o'clock," said Dawlish, "and if I'm not there, wait for me?"

"You are extremely kind," murmured the tramp. "I will do that if you will be good enough to tell me where *Four Ways* is, and how I get to it—and perhaps, if you will be so good, tell me your name. I have not entirely lost faith in human nature, but I have known people who, when they see me arrive, refuse to believe that I have an appointment with the master of the house."

"They'll believe you," said Dawlish confidently. "And if you turn left at the foot of the hill, then left again, walk through the village and take the right hand fork at the end of it, you will find *Four Ways*, half-way up the hill."

The tramp looked at him and, then, somewhat sadly, looked at the car. He hesitated, and then asked:

"Are you going to be *very* long?" He raised a dilapidated foot. "I am a little footsore."

Dawlish grinned. "All right, I'll give you a lift if you'll wait. But first, about this man who was wearing this hat. Was he standing here?"

"Just inside the thicket," said the tramp. "I doubt whether I would have seen him but for the imprecation, which drew my attention. I went forward to see whether I could help, and, when I saw the trivial nature of the mishap, exchanged the time of day and walked on. I did not feel that I was welcome here. Are you interested in the man?"

"I'm interested in all inexplicable things," Dawlish said lightly.

"And you find this incident inexplicable?"

"Enough to be a little curious as to where the hatless man has gone."

Dawlish entered the thicket, the strange wayfarer by his side. He was worried. The hat had certainly not been thrown up there in exasperation. He felt sure by now that this hat belonged to Leven's policeman. Leven had explained that the three points were manned day and night, the watchers moving nearer to *Akers* after dark. It was hardly dusk yet, so it was unlikely that this man had taken a forward position. The hat was a puzzle. Why had it been tossed up on the tree? There was one possible explanation: it could have been thrown there for no other reason than to attract attention. The fact that the watcher wasn't in sight, and on duty, suggested that he had been forced to leave. If Alderney—or anyone interested in Alderney—wanted to make sure that the house was not watched from that particular point, they might have taken him away.

Dawlish thought of Flash Ben's corpse.

There were cigarette ends beneath a tree on the edge of the thicket. From there, it was possible to see the house clearly. This was the point where the man had stationed himself. One thing interested Dawlish particularly: four little holes in the earth, making a rectangle about a foot long by nine inches wide. A stool had been placed there.

Dawlish examined the position with care.

The tramp observed him with a certain mild benignity.

"One would almost think that you had reason to believe that the man was observing Alderney House," he observed at last.

"Doesn't the evidence point to it?" asked Dawlish. "Do you know exactly what time it was when you passed here?"

"I am afraid that I have no watch, sir, but I would say—let me see! A bus passed the end of the road as I turned into it, and I distinctly recall that it had *Godalming* on the front. What time would such a bus pass the corner?"

Dawlish said slowly: "One leaves the village at seven o'clock."

"And how long does it take to get here?"

"About ten minutes," Dawlish said.

"And it would take me, perhaps, another five to walk from the end of the road. Then I saw him here at quarter past seven. A point satisfactorily cleared up, although, it can hardly be a matter of importance."

"You might be wrong about that," said Dawlish.

A trail of broken twigs and trodden leaves betrayed the fact that several men had been in the thicket recently, and Dawlish imagined that they had crept upon the watching policeman, overpowered him and carried him off. This reasoning, Dawlish knew, might be badly out; the man might have gone away on some inquiry or even to telephone a report to his headquarters, but—there was the hat.

Dawlish looked up.

If it had been thrown up in the air just on the edge of the little hidey-hole, it would have lodged in that particular tree. There had been a scuffle; and the policeman had tossed his hat away, to give an indication that something was amiss.

Leven must be informed at once.

There was an A.A. box on the corner of the road; he would have to use that, for he could hardly telephone from Alderney's house and thus let it be known that he knew it was being watched.

Looking at *Akers* through the gap in the thicket, Dawlish suddenly saw a cloud of smoke rising from the roof.

"There appears to be a fire," said the tramp, gently.

A suspicion that the tramp might know more about the fire than appeared on the surface, occurred sharply to Dawlish as he bundled the man into his car and headed for the A.A. box.

In less than five seconds he was talking to an attentive sergeant at the Haslemere Police Station.

"First, your man at Short Hill has disappeared," Dawlish

reported, "second, there seems to be a fire at *Akers*. Please inform the fire station, and pass on what I have told you to Inspector Leven as soon as possible."

"At once, sir."

Dawlish, driving at a furious pace, was half-way towards the house when the tramp spoke again.

"Surely someone at the house will have reported the fire," he observed.

"Such an assumption has been the cornerstone of many a tragedy," said Dawlish sententiously. He swung between the posts of the open gateway leading to the house, and then along the rough drive; this was a secondary entrance. For some minutes they had been unable to see anything but the road on which they were travelling, but as they passed a row of beeches, the house came into sight. Above the west wing a cloud of dark smoke hovered.

There was no sight or sound of a fire engine.

As they drew nearer, Dawlish saw several men moving about the garden. Suddenly the evening sun glinted on a jet of water which shot towards the flames; the amateur house firemen were at work. It was possible that Alderney had decided to leave the firefighting to his own staff.

Dawlish saw that the road turned sharply a little further along, and took the turn wide but without slowing down appreciably. As he swung round, he glimpsed the branch of a tree stretching across their path.

With a furious "Look out!" he jammed on the brakes.

The warning came too late for the tramp to do anything about it. His head banged on the windscreen. The car jolted to a standstill.

The tramp straightened up, and rubbed his forehead gingerly.

"What an extraordinary thing," he remarked.

"Most," said Dawlish. He measured the distance between the branch and the trees bordering the drive; it was impossible to squeeze through. "Lend me a hand," he added, and jumped out. The tramp followed, a little unsteadily. Dawlish glanced at him, and saw that the blow had been a heavy one.

Why should anyone want to delay traffic there?

As Dawlish took one end of the branch, and the tramp the other, Dawlish thought of one possibility: the fire engine coming from Haslemere would take that drive; if someone had wanted the engine to crash, to assure the fire getting a stronger hold, a blocked road would be the answer.

Dawlish started the car again very thoughtfully.

Once they were clear of the copse, the house seemed very near. The smoke rose in a black column until it was high in the sky. A dozen or so men were standing near the corner which was afire, and the one pitifully thin water jet was having little or no effect on the flames.

Two or three men looked round towards the car. One shouted: "Have you seen the fire engine?"

"It's coming," called Dawlish. He thought he saw Alderney directing the fire-fighters. Two women were standing on the fringe of the little crowd. A line had been formed and buckets of water were passing from hand to hand, to feed the tank which fed the hose. The smell of burning was sharp in his nostrils, and the roar of the fire was clearly audible.

One of the women turned towards him, and he saw that it was Lady Alderney.

"Mr. Dawlish!"

"No one's trapped, I hope."

"I—we don't think so," said Janice Alderney. "We don't really know, it got such a hold before anyone discovered it."

As she spoke, there was a distant sound of fire-bells, and the woman appeared to relax.

"I thought it would never get here!"

Dawlish said: "How can we make sure no one's trapped?"

"Brian's trying to find out."

"Inside?"

"Yes, he—"

Dawlish turned towards the front door. Janice Alderney hurried after him. She caught up with him in the hall, and led the way up the wide staircase, then along a landing towards a second staircase. Here the crackle of burning was very loud. No one was in sight on the first floor, but Dawlish saw two men on the second. A little way beyond them the flames were licking their way along a narrow passage.

Alderney was one of the men.

"Anything I can do?" Dawlish asked.

Alderney looked round. Dawlish was startled by the sight of his set, angry face, the glitter in his eyes. This was a different Alderney. He showed no surprise at seeing Dawlish, and said in a clipped voice:

"If anyone's in there, he's had it."

"Surely you know."

Alderney said in a searing voice:

"I *don't* know. When the devil is that fire engine coming?"

"It's almost here," said Dawlish. "We might get this carpet up, the fire will travel along it." He went nearer the flames taking a knife from his pocket. Alderney joined him, and between them they hacked the carpet from wall to wall, and then rolled it back. The other man had gone off with Lady Alderney.

Alderney said: "One day, I'll—" and then he broke off abruptly, and smiled. There was no humour in the smile; and again Dawlish thought that he was looking at a different man. "It could be worse," Alderney went on, abruptly. "It'll be confined to this wing—and the vaults."

"Vaults?"

"It started down there," said Alderney, and gave a harsh laugh. "This is a much better show than the one on the road, Dawlish."

Dawlish did not speak.

Men came hurrying up the stairs, dragging a hose with them, and soon water was spraying on the walls and the floor. The flames seemed to have too strong a hold to be extinguished easily, but after some minutes it was obvious that they were being held. Alderney rubbed his hands wearily over his face, and led the way downstairs.

A footman appeared in the hall.

"Is there anything I can do, sir?"

"Get something to drink for everyone outside," Alderney said. "I can do with a drink myself," he added, as he led Dawlish into a small room, lined with books, and busied himself with bottles and glasses.

"Beer, I think," he murmured.

"Yes, thanks," Dawlish was already parched.

Alderney's hand was steady as he poured out. He drank deeply, but thought to raise his glass to Dawlish. For the first time that evening, there was a faint hint of the mocking smile which Dawlish had seen before.

Alderney put down the empty glass, and said slowly:

"Someone was to have seen me this evening, and should have been waiting in the room where the fire got the strongest hold."

"Oh," said Dawlish.

"He may have escaped, I don't know."

"Shouldn't we find out?"

"I sent a man to do that," said Alderney. "Still, there's no point in staying here. Another?"

"No, thanks."

Three fire-fighting units were by now engaged, one with its snake-like hose running through windows and across a large sitting-room to the stairs, the others playing on the fire from the outside. Although the centre of the fire was still a fierce red, there was no further danger of it spreading.

The footman had got to work quickly. A man was carrying out a small barrel of beer, another was bringing a huge can of water, a third some bottles of fruit cordials. It was astonishing efficiency; and Dawlish was surprised, among other things, by the fact that Alderney had thought of providing something to drink.

Viewed at close quarters, the damage was extensive. Standing back and surveying the house itself, it was seen in better perspective. The greater part of the house would show no signs of there having been a fire.

An escape was run up to the second floor, and a man began to direct a jet of water through a window.

He turned suddenly, and signalled.

Chapter 7

UNKNOWN VICTIM

Dawlish watched the scene with quickening pulse. Alderney had joined his wife, and they were watching with tense interest. The fire-fighters seemed to ignore this sudden drama, and to carry on with what they were doing—and the footman calmly continued to put glasses on the table, and to erect the barrel of beer on two small trestles.

Two men stood at the top of the escape, while the man who had signalled the alarm directed water into the room. One of the others climbed in. He seemed to be out of sight for a long time.

Dawlish held his breath.

They were lifting something out.

It was unrecognisable from where Dawlish was standing, but the men were taking astonishing care. The burden was lifted into a tarpaulin sheet, and lowered down the ladder.

The firemen's sober care and solemnity were unmistakable.

Lady Alderney exclaimed: "Oh, Brian!"

A woman began to sob.

Dawlish watched Alderney, who stared up with set face. It

was impossible to judge what the man was thinking. Dawlish glanced at the fireman descending the ladder. It was possible, now, to see that he carried a body. The arms were hanging over the man's back. Long hair dropped forward, swaying as the man moved.

A voice spoke near Dawlish.

"What a terrible thing!"

It was the tramp; and Dawlish, who had forgotten him, looked down in some surprise. The little man's face was ashen.

Dawlish said nothing.

The Chief Fire Officer walked to Alderney, and asked something which Dawlish did not hear. Alderney's answer was loud enough.

"The summer house, I think."

"Very good, sir."

As soon as the body was out of sight, Alderney followed, and Dawlish fell into step with him. They entered the summer house together. The Chief Officer and another man were bending over the victim; no one needed telling that the woman was dead. The sheet was over her legs and waist, but enough was visible to make Alderney draw in a sharp breath. Dawlish tightened his lips.

Only her face seemed to have escaped.

The Chief Officer straightened up.

"We want a doctor," he said, and turned round. "Will one of you telephone the police, please? I must get back to the fire." He pushed his way out, and as he passed, Dawlish heard him say: "Poor kid!"

Dawlish touched his arm.

"Poor what?"

"She's little more than a girl," said the Chief Officer, and hurried off, as if he did not want to talk.

Alderney took a cigarette-case from his pocket, and lit a cigarette without offering one to Dawlish. He seemed oblivious of Dawlish and of the fireman who had been left on duty. He stared at the charred, blackened figure. His lips were working; and Dawlish saw with astonishment that there were tears in his eyes.

Alderney turned away abruptly.

In the hall, he telephoned Haslemere police station; when that was done, he went into the book-lined room again, and this time he helped himself to a whisky and soda. He motioned to the decanter, with a silent 'help yourself'. Dawlish did so. Alderney went to the window, and looked out.

This room was far removed from the scene of the fire, and overlooked a flower-garden and trim lawns, much larger than the lawns at *Four Ways*. There seemed nothing here to disturb the lovely country scene.

Alderney did not speak.

Then the door opened and his wife came in.

Dawlish was determined to stay with Alderney as long as he could. Now, he transferred his attention to Janice Alderney. She was deathly white, her hands moving before her unsteadily. She took a step towards Alderney, and Alderney put down his glass and went to her. In a moment she was in his arms, crying bitterly.

"Do you mind leaving us, Dawlish?" Alderney asked.

There was nothing else to be done. Dawlish went out, carrying with him a picture of that stricken face, Lady Alderney's sobs still echoing in his ears.

It was half-past ten, and quite dark, before Dawlish reached home. The tramp was sitting by his side.

"Are you sure I won't be in the way?"

"There's a room over the garage," Dawlish said. "Make yourself comfortable there."

"You are very kind."

"And collect a snack from the kitchen," Dawlish said.

He went first to the kitchen and told Chloe what to do, and then walked towards the front room. The others, he had seen through the window, were all sitting together. Felicity leapt to her feet, her astonishment tinged with resignation. Dawlish did not realise that he was covered with black smears, his hair awry, his coat carrying the acrid stench of scorch.

"What's happened?" Felicity asked quietly.

"I'll tell you all together," Dawlish said.

He was able, now, to fill in many details which he had learned since Alderney had asked him to leave him alone with his wife. He had talked with Leven and the Chief Fire Officer as well as Alderney.

But Alderney had not talked freely; and Dawlish did not think he had told the truth.

According to his story, he was about to employ a secretary, and a girl had come to interview him that evening. He did not explain why such a time should be chosen for an interview, nor why the girl had gone to that particular room. The fact that a girl had called was corroborated by two members of the staff; and Leven had made sure that none of the staff concerned had recognised her. Asked for details of the arrangement for the interview, Alderney had said that all the correspondence had been in the room where the girl had died. Leven had been particularly inquisitive about the self-locking door, but it had been one of several at *Akers*.

Dawlish believed there was a lot more to be said.

The fire certainly seemed to have started in two places at once—in the vaults, immediately beneath the west wing which had suffered in the fire, and on the second floor, where the girl had been trapped. This part of the house was not used as living quarters, although Alderney used several of the rooms as 'offices'. He did not explain why part of *Akers* was used for business purposes; in fact his reticence was remarkable.

The cause of the fire was as yet unknown, although Alderney advanced one theory which appeared to be plausible. He was keen on amateur cine-pictures, and in the vaults and in the offices stored a large number of films.

"And according to him, 'something' set them off," said Dawlish. "That's as far as we've got yet, but I think he knows a lot more."

"What does Leven think."

"The same as I do, but Leven is prejudiced against Alderney," Dawlish said.

"Well, naturally," murmured Beresford. "Prejudice is always prejudice when indulged in by Leven. In us, of course, it's a well-founded conviction."

Dawlish laughed. "Certainly I still believe Alderney knows a good deal more than he's told, but that doesn't mean that I don't see his good points. I liked his manner tonight. And I know he was badly upset about what happened. It won't surprise me if he comes over tomorrow," he said. "He knows that I saw more than anyone else, and he may be worried by it. I stayed with him until the police told me to go."

"Was his wife affected?" asked Felicity.

"Very much so."

Tim Jeremy rubbed a wrinkled forehead.

"So you think Alderney started the fire himself?"

"I do not," said Dawlish, firmly. "It shocked him far too much. I should say that two or three people raided the house and started it, that the watching policeman was put out of the way so that he could not report certain visitors to the house, that someone broke into the vaults, and—"

He paused, abruptly.

"The great man's had an idea," murmured Ted.

Dawlish rubbed the bridge of his nose.

"Well, how's this for one," he agreed. "The vaults were electrically controlled, which is quite usual these days. If someone started some funny business, there might have been a short-circuit, which could in turn have started the fire. The experts will be able to tell us about that in a day or two. It's the most likely thing I can think of."

"It wouldn't start the fire in both places," reasoned Ted.

"No." Dawlish leaned back and closed his eyes. "I suppose guessing won't get us anywhere."

"It's time someone did a bit more than guessing," said Tim, with spirit. "We haven't been told whether any of the prisoners we took last night have talked. And—" he wagged a finger at Dawlish—"you haven't explained why you brought a tramp home with you."

"Oh," said Dawlish, and smiled. "No, I haven't."

He told them about the tramp, the reference to 'Alderney House' and his conviction that the man was rather more than he appeared to be. He agreed with Tim and Ted that it was also possible he knew something about the fire.

"After all," said Tim, "he admitted that he'd been to the house. It's so easy to start a fire, these days—you only need a thimbleful of the right stuff, and you can have a merry blaze in five minutes."

Dawlish rubbed one smear off his face and created another. "I'll have a word with the police on duty and tell them to keep their eyes on the garage during the night."

"We might do a spot of watching ourselves," said Tim.

"I don't think that will be necessary," Dawlish said, "we'll be called if there's anything the matter. An early night wouldn't do any of us any harm. And tomorrow's Sunday. It might be a quiet day."

"My dear chap!" exclaimed Timothy, shocked. "A quiet day?—what's that?"

"Oh, the chief agents of all this upheaval will probably lie low for a bit now." Dawlish paused. "I wonder if we can find a connection between tonight's business and the hold-ups. They *might* be quite unconnected."

"What a hope," said Timothy.

It was on that not very satisfactory note that they separated to go to bed.

Dawlish had spoken to the watching police, and been assured that an eye would be kept on the tramp, nevertheless he thought he'd better have a last look at him before turning in. A number of things about the tramp had seemed odd and surprising. Here was another, more odd and surprising than the rest:

He was wearing a pair of clean pyjamas.

The next morning passed quietly.

No one called. At half-past ten, Felicity and Joan went to the village church. The men gathered in the morning-room and discussed the mystery; it was a purposeless kind of session in one way, but it did enable Dawlish to get his thoughts clear; and he came to the conclusion that the fire and the thefts could not be unconnected.

Leven and a fire-assessor visited *Akers* during the afternoon. It had been accepted that the fire had started in the two places. The films, completely destroyed, were possibly the primary cause. There was evidence of short-circuiting in the vault, but none in the upstairs room.

Leven had questioned the staff at the house again, and had got the same results: The girl had been completely unknown to them. She had been waiting to see Alderney for twenty minutes before the fire had been discovered. Alderney and his wife had been walking in the grounds, and were on their way back after being told that the girl, who had given her name as Mary Keen, had arrived. Until then, everything at the house had appeared normal, nor was there any evidence that the house had been broken into. The five members of the indoor staff and the three gardeners had been in the servants' wing; the main quarters had been empty, as the Alderneys had been in the garden. Directly the fire was discovered, Alderney had telephoned to the fire station and then gone upstairs to see the girl; he had been forced back by the flames.

Dawlish remembered his bleak expression; and the half-truth that he had told.

Had he thought it possible that the girl had escaped before the fire took a hold?

Thinking over the events of the evening, Dawlish came to the conclusion that he might have hoped she had, but had not really thought it likely.

Why had his wife been so affected?

Who was the girl?

"That's going to be our main trouble," Leven said, breaking into Dawlish's thoughts, "identifying the girl, I mean. All Alderney can tell us is that she came from London. He says he didn't make a note of her address and can't remember the name of the street or district. I suppose that's reasonable enough."

"Or plausible," Dawlish said.

"If you ask me, Alderney knows a lot more about this than he admits," Leven said. "We've asked the Yard to try to trace the girl, of course—there'll be a mention in the six o'clock news tonight, and photographs in the papers tomorrow. Poor kid."

Dawlish changed the subject.

The prisoners from the hold-up, it appeared, were uncommunicative. Leven thought that in the case of two of the men, it was simply that they knew little. They were members of a well-known London criminal gang, with records a yard long. In neither case were they greatly perturbed about being caught, they were used to prison life and—Leven said—it was almost certain that their wives and families would be looked after during their 'holiday'.

The third man was in a different category.

He had no police record. His manner was not sullen or resentful; merely bland in his refusal to talk.

The two old lags had been assured that there was a 'picking' at Haslemere. Details were to be given to them, when they reached the town. They had been met by a man called Rummy, who had told them that they were to take part in a hold-up. Neither of them had been reluctant, their chief concern being their rake-off, which, they were given to understand, would be a handsome one.

None of the three admitted knowing that Flash Ben had been in the neighbourhood.

"Why they brought him here, I just can't guess," Leven said, "unless it was to frighten you—and if that was the case, it just doesn't make sense that Alderney begged you to take part in the chase."

"It'll work out," Dawlish said, briskly. "I could make a guess about Flash Ben."

"Go ahead," said Leven.

"He was going to squeal," said Dawlish. "He wasn't satisfied with his cut over earlier jobs or his promise in this one, and he was either coming to see me or you, to give us the low-down. Probably he was foolish enough to threaten this. Bye-bye, Flash Ben! Had he a family?"

"A wife and five kids," said Leven.

"Is Trivett seeing the wife?"

"I expect so," Leven said.

Trivett, who telephoned a little later in the afternoon, said that he had seen Flash Ben's wife, but that all she professed to know was that he was 'doing a job' in the country. Trivett, who knew the underworld as few men did, thought that she might talk more freely a little later.

"It depends whether she's looked after," he said. "If the people who killed Flash Ben give her a pension for a year or two, she won't complain. If they cut her off, she'll get nasty. I think they'll pay her."

Dawlish told his friends of that conversation after tea, when Leven and the fire-assessor had gone. No one seemed surprised, except Anne.

"Did you say *pension*, Pat?"

Dawlish smiled at her. "Yes."

"Surely these gangs aren't as well organised as that?"

"It's a long story," Dawlish said. "Gangs don't work as a unit in everything. It's a loose kind of arrangement. A man might be a member of a gang but work almost entirely on his own, with a few cronies. These little cliques know when they can get help for a job they can't handle themselves—they might want half a dozen for a smash-and-grab raid, and be only three strong. So, they call on others of the 'gang'. There's a leader, but he doesn't issue orders as a general rule, he's just the most successful rogue of the lot—the man who seldom gets caught. When someone does get caught, it's a matter of honour for the others to look after his family until he comes out. Hence, the 'pension'."

"It sounds to me mighty like a trade union," Anne said grimly.

Dawlish said slowly: "Substitute 'crime' for 'trade' and you're not far wrong. At least they're as highly organised. If you'd like me to guess, I would say that there are half a dozen people leading them, and they employ others from the various London gangs as and when they think fit. There might be another series of hold-ups tonight, or any night next week. With a few exceptions, the same men wouldn't be used in it. That would be too dangerous."

"Why?"

"The police probably know several of the men who were working on Friday," Dawlish told her, "and those people and their friends are being watched. If they were to leave their usual haunts they would be followed—in the same way as Flash Ben and Rummy were followed. The police might lose some of them, but they certainly wouldn't lose them all. Besides, the men who did Friday's job have had their rake-off by now—probably a hundred pounds apiece. It might even be more. They won't want to work while they're well off. Some of them will spend down to their last pound before they start off on another job. Some keep a float of thirty or forty pounds, and start work when they're down to that level, but with a few exceptions—the leaders—they don't go in for big money."

"You make it horribly realistic," Anne said.

"It's realistic all right," said Dawlish. "The trouble just now is that someone is using these gangs pretty cleverly. Probably the fence."

"Fence?"

"Precious," murmured Tim, "would you like to come for a walk round the orchard, and I'll introduce you to the elementary principles of professional crime."

"I'd much rather hear from Pat," said Anne.

"Such loyalty," said Tim. "Go on, oracle."

Dawlish smiled. "Don't underrate Anne's technique. She's simply humouring the male love of showing off, bless her." He stirred restlessly in his chair. "You can take my word that a fence of some pretensions is working this all right. There's no blinking the fact that there's a pretty powerful directing intelligence behind it."

"Have you given Alderney up?"

"Not yet," said Dawlish. "I—"

He broke off, for from outside there came the shrill blast of a police whistle.

He was out of his chair like a shot, racing for the open door, Tim and Beresford close behind him. The whistle blew again— and it was followed by a high-pitched shout.

Chapter 8

DAWLISH GETS A KNOCK

The policeman blowing his whistle was running along the drive towards the back of the house. It was from there the cry had come. Dawlish, with Tim on his heels, raced in close pursuit. He could hear shouts, and sounds of violent confusion, coming from the open windows of the room above the garage.

Men were struggling inside.

Dawlish saw the face of the tramp. A man was clutching his throat, and the tramp's eyes were starting from his head. He had stopped screaming now, but someone else was shouting, as if in pain. Dawlish reached the steps leading up to the room, and, on the platform at the top, saw a policeman huddled against the railings, waving his hands.

Half-way up the steps, Dawlish realised that he was trying to convey a warning; someone was at the door.

He vaulted over the railings. It was a long drop to the ground, but he reached it without losing his balance, and then rushed towards the window. Beneath it was a rain-water butt. Dawlish put a foot on the side of the butt, grabbed the pipe which fed it, and hauled himself to an upright position. He could hear hoarse panting from inside the room, but was below the level of the window sill, and could not see inside. He stretched upwards, on tip-toe.

He slipped.

His right leg went under water, almost to the knee, but recovering his foothold he stretched up again. He reached the window sill.

The tramp was still struggling, but his face was mottled, and agonised.

"*What can we do?*" cried Felicity, from below.

"Get guns!" called Dawlish.

He wished he had not spoken, for the man who had the tramp in that dreadful stranglehold, glanced round. Dawlish pulled himself up with one knee on the sill. The man inside flung the tramp away from him, and jumped towards Dawlish. Dawlish struck out wildly, still in danger of losing his balance. He caught the man on the nose, and made him back away in sudden pain. Dawlish clutched the inside of the window, and managed to get a leg inside. As he did so, the other man rushed at him, and Dawllsh, just able to see the man's upraised arm, felt a sudden fierce pain just below his knee. Dawlish got his other leg inside, but when he put his right foot to the ground, the leg doubled up under him. He clutched the windowsill, in a desperate attempt to keep his balance.

It was then he saw the flash of a knife.

Dawlish waited.

There was a moment of silence; even the scuffling by the door did not seem to break it. Dawlish crouched, his right foot just touching the floor, all his weight on his left. The man sprang.

Dawlish went forward at the same time, striking at the man's right wrist. The knife grazed the back of his hand, then the arm was thrust to one side.

Footsteps sounded close to them.

"O.K.," said Tim, "leave it to me."

Dawlish stood back, resting against the wall. Tim weighed in. There was a frightening efficiency about him when he went into action; and just then he was white with anger. He wrenched the knife out of the assailant's hand, flung it aside, and then struck him with quick rights and lefts to the face and chest. Under the storm of blows, the man backed away, until he could go no further. Dawlish saw the man fall.

"That'll do," he called.

"Right." Tim stepped back. The sudden onslaught had eased his anger, and he grinned. "How are you?"

"I'll do," said Dawlish. "Any harm done outside?"

"Plenty," said Tim, "but nothing fatal, I think."

"Then it could be worse," said Dawlish. "Have a go at him, will you?" He nodded to the tramp.

That little man lay on the floor, unconscious, his face now ashen. Tim bent down, lifted him, and laid him gently on the bed.

Dawlish limped to the knife, and picked it up. Near it was a piece of lead piping, the weapon which had hurt his knee. He heard Felicity and one of the other women on the steps leading to the room, and hobbled across to the door.

The policeman was still half lying on the landing, his face white with pain. Beresford had taken off the man's boot and sock. There was an ugly bruise on the instep, discoloured and swollen. The other policeman was at the foot of the steps, holding a second stranger in his powerful grip. Dawlish realised what had happened; one man had been on guard at the door— as he had understood from the policeman's warning signal— and Tim and the second policeman had rushed him, and had some difficulty in overpowering him in the cramped space. But he was under arrest now, and the policeman below was making sure that he did not get away.

Dawlish looked keenly about the grounds. He could see no sign of anyone else being present, but there were small clumps of trees behind which men might hide. He watched one which seemed to be swaying a great deal, and then decided that it was due to the wind and a flock of birds.

Beresford straightened up.

"Well, Pat?"

"I'm not really surprised," said Dawlish, "but I expected them to act by night, if they acted at all. A sense of urgency prevails."

They moved back into the room, and Beresford went immediately to the bed. Dawlish went down on his good knee, to look at the tramp's face. It was a more natural colour.

"He'll be all right," said Dawlish, confidently.

He went to the window and called down to the policeman to keep a watch on the back of the house. The man nodded. Dawlish leaned against the window, wishing that the pain in his knee would ease. He did not want to relax until he felt sure that there was no risk of another attack.

None developed.

Leven arrived a little more than half an hour later, bringing with him several men; Dawlish was beginning to respect Leven's constant preparedness. It was a relief to let the police take over, and a relief to feel Felicity's hand on his arm, and hear her say:

"Now I'm going to have a look at your knee."

The knee was swollen and discoloured, but the doctor was confident that nothing was broken. Dawlish, he said, would have to rest the leg for a few days; after that, he should be as right as rain. He pronounced the same verdict about the injured policeman, and he prescribed a warm bed and hot coffee for the tramp, who had recovered consciousness but was still limp and silent. The doctor went off, Leven's men took the two prisoners away, the guard in the house was doubled, and then Leven entered the drawing-room, where Dawlish was sitting with his leg propped up on cushions.

"You're seeing life," he said laconically. "You always thought there was something odd about the tramp, didn't you?"

"I have my methods," said Dawlish, with a grin. "By the way, you did agree with Trivett officially asking me to lend a hand, didn't you?"

"I certainly did," Leven assured him. "When a show like this is on, it would be criminal to let you pick apples!"

Felicity's eyebrows rose expressively.

"My wife is prejudiced," declared Dawlish, and grimaced at her. "The general idea was that I should tackle Alderney, and I still hope to do that. Until then, I'd like to tackle the tramp—my own way."

"Oh," said Leven, and the smile faded.

"I'd like to keep him here until the morning," said Dawlish, "and then see what he has to say. I've a feeling that he will be more amenable with me than with you. Are there any real objections?"

After a long pause, Leven said slowly:

"Well, have it your own way."

"Now that is handsome of you," declared Dawlish. "Have a drink."

"No thanks," said Leven, seriously. He looked rather troubled, and obviously would have been happier to take the tramp into Haslemere for formal questioning. Having reached his decision, however, he made no attempt to change it.

Dawlish asked if there were any news of 'Mary Keen'. Nothing had yet been heard from London, it proved, but there was one item of information which obviously gave Leven considerable pleasure. The man who had been watching *Akers* from Short Hill had been found, tied hand and foot in an old barn on the edge of a farm not a mile away from the vantage point. His story was simple enough. A car had pulled up, three men from it had distracted his attention, and then he had been attacked from behind. He had no chance to defend himself, said Leven, and added with a smile:

"But he managed to toss his hat into the tree."

"Nicely done," murmured Dawlish. "I wonder if the men went on to *Akers*."

"Not only that, but they probably started the fire, in my opinion," said Leven. "It's a bit odd that they weren't observed, but it isn't difficult to approach *Akers* without being seen until you're right on the place."

Leven looked at Dawlish thoughtfully.

"You don't think Alderney connived at the fire, do you?"

"I don't know what to think," admitted Dawlish, "but I do feel that the hold-ups, the fire and the attack on the tramp are all connected."

"That's pretty clear," agreed Leven, and went on: "You know what I think of Alderney, but the fellow would hardly set fire to his own house. When will you have another shot at him?"

"As soon as I can get about," Dawlish promised, and then asked casually: "Any more jewel robberies?"

"Nothing since Friday," said Leven. He heaved himself out of his chair. "I'll let you know at once where the tramp's attackers came from."

He was too optimistic, however. He telephoned later in the evening, to tell Dawlish that neither of the men had police records, neither had anything in their possession to give a clue to their identity, and both admitted to the name of Smith. They were, in Leven's opinion, in a category between that of the old lags caught after the hold-up and the one man who had been consistent in his refusal to talk. And he was sure that, had they been members of any known gang, the Yard would have had their finger-prints.

"The thing I like least about this business is the beggars without a record," Leven said. "It's downright sinister."

"I fully agree with you, old chap. Does Trivett know about the latest development?"

"He certainly does."

"Well, it will all come out in the wash," said Dawlish comfortably, adding with a laugh in his voice: "We hope. I'll let you know in the event of another emergency!"

He replaced the receiver, and looked out of the window. He was, on Felicity's instructions, in bed, and all the others were downstairs—except the tramp, who had been put in one of the smaller bedrooms.

Dawlish brooded over the tramp.

He had felt sure, from the beginning, that there was a mystery about the man, but until the attack on him, he had thought that the tramp might be trying to get into *Four Ways* as a spy. I was all very confusing. Left for an hour on his own, hearing only a murmur of voices downstairs, Dawlish worried over the affair, but came to no conclusion. Then he heard sounds of the party breaking up. Soon there was a chorus of good-nights, and at last Felicity came in. She drew the curtains, and switched on the main light, then sat on the dressing-table stool and looked at Dawlish intently.

"Yes, I am alive," murmured Dawlish.

"You hardly deserve to be," said Felicity, soberly.

"Only indirectly," said Dawlish, meekly. "What's been going on downstairs?"

"Plans and counter-plans," said Felicity. "Anne has to go back in the morning, and Joan doesn't want to be away from the children any longer. So Tim's going to drive them both back, and is returning in the afternoon. Ted's staying on. And then I suppose the three of you will put your heads together and hatch some crazy scheme to get to the bottom of all this."

"In an advisory capacity only," Dawlish said, mildly.

"Advisory or not," said Felicity sceptically, "*you* will be out of it for the better part of a week." She patted Dawlish's unwounded knee. "I do want the whole thing to be over quickly. Will it be all right if I go and see Lady Alderney in the morning?"

After a pause, Dawlish said:

"I don't see why not. I can't imagine there'll be any danger at *Akers* just now. Since the fire, I gather that Leven's been watching the place much more closely, without caring whether Alderney knows or likes it. You'll be all right. What line will you take?"

"I don't know until I get there," Felicity said, and her eyes danced.

Dawlish felt a little depressed. It was one thing for him to get cracking, quite another for Felicity to take an active part. He had wanted to keep her out of it, but saw how inevitable it was that she should at last be drawn in. Still worrying about it, he went to sleep.

Tim, Anne and Joan left a little after ten o'clock next morning. Dawlish hobbled to the window and waved to them, then went back to a chair by the bed, and looked at his swollen, bandaged knee. It was stiff and painful, and Felicity was probably right when she said it would be a week before he was about again in real earnest. And events were likely to move quickly.

Ted came in soon afterwards.

"How's it going?" he asked.

"I can see the whole shindy being over before I can do

anything about it," said Dawlish, gloomily. "No news of any kind, I suppose?"

Beresford chuckled.

"A little. Your tramp is asking for you. Will you go to him, or shall I bring him in here?"

Chapter 9

THE APOLOGETIC TRAMP

"My dear sir," said the tramp, looking up from the bed on which he was resting, "I am so very sorry about this—indeed, words fail me, Mr. Dawlish."

He glanced at the bandaged knee, winced, and "I cannot forgive myself," he said, "I really cannot. I can only offer you my most sincere apologies."

Dawlish smiled, and studied the man with increasing interest. He did not look like one who was a stranger to good living. His voice, through all his vicissitudes, had retained a mellow, cultured tone. His hands, Dawlish saw, were small, with long, well-kept fingers.

"The police," the little man murmured, "so diligent at questioning. I have been waiting for them."

"They've agreed to leave that to me," Dawlish informed him.

"Indeed."

"So here I am."

"I give you my assurance, sir, that I shall answer to the very best of my ability. Have no fear of that. I am only too anxious to help."

"Good!" said Dawlish. "What's your name?"

The little man hesitated.

He looked a little crestfallen, as if he were disappointed that he had to hesitate at the first question. He blinked, and glanced at Beresford. Perhaps he was contrasting the bulk of Beresford and the size of Dawlish with his own frail body. He was certainly not frightened, however, and after a while a smile curved his lips.

"I am sorely tempted to lie to you, but I will not," he said. "I bear an honoured name, though there are those who think that I have shamed it. My name is Fripp."

Dawlish sat up. Beresford's glance sharpened.

"A relative of Lady Fripp?"

"Her only close relative—her nephew."

"I see," said Dawlish.

"I have not been in Haslemere for many years," the tramp went on, "and I feel sure that I would not be easily recognised even by my aunt or very close acquaintances. Colonel Maitland certainly did not recognise me."

He paused, but neither of the others spoke.

"What is your next question?" asked Fripp.

Many were flooding Dawlish's mind, but just then there seemed no justification for questioning the man about hispast.

"Why have you come to this district?" he asked.

"It is so long since I have been here, and I felt a nostalgia for the place. You can understand how its loveliness appeals to a native, I am sure."

"You did promise to tell me the truth, didn't you?" asked Dawlish.

"That *is* the truth," said Fripp earnestly. "There are supplementary reasons, but I assure you that I would in any case have returned here. Will it shock you, Mr. Dawlish, if I tell you that I have spent several years in prison?"

Dawlish's eyes crinkled at the corners.

"Not a bit."

"Somehow I felt that it would not," said Fripp. "I spent my time—five years in all—in different jails, but mostly in Parkmoor. I will not go into the details of the life I led there, but there are some things which I feel will interest you. For instance, the amount that one *learns* in prison. I was astonished! There is a fraternity among criminals which is quite remarkable. Even inside prisons, they are divided, there are reliable men who can be trusted by the inmates and the—ah—squealers, upon whom revenge is sometimes taken. There are the trustworthy warders—trustworthy, I mean, from the point of view of the convict. But these facts are probably known to you."

"More or less," said Dawlish.

"There are two other features about prison life which surprised me," said Fripp. "The first is the fact that these men, these convicts, are completely without any sense of shame or guilt—and they look forward, with eager anticipation to the time when they can 'get busy' again. Many good people, I believe, think that prisons are preventive institutions. They are not. Plans for the future are *quite* the most important factor in the lives of the majority of convicts. Did you know that?"

"I've heard it said," murmured Dawlish.

"Would you be surprised to know that I met *two* people who owed their sentences largely to you and your friends?"

"Not really surprised," said Dawlish.

"I am glad to tell you that neither of them nurses a grievance," Fripp told him calmly. "They consider that you fight fairly—oh, that is another interesting thing. They classify policeman. There is a certain Scotland Yard man—Trivett, by name—" Fripp paused for a moment, but neither of the others moved—"who is rated very high. In fact many of the men are fond of him. On the other hand, others at Scotland Yard are extremely unpopular. On the whole, however, the provincial police are disliked more than those in London." Fripp raised his eyebrows. "I do hope I am not boring you, Mr. Dawlish."

"Not a bit," said Dawlish.

"I'm so glad. And this is not without its purpose," Fripp went on. "I heard, while I was in Parkmoor, that for many years there has been a fence, a receiver of stolen goods, of some standing living in this part of the world."

"For how many years?" asked Dawlish.

"I cannot say precisely, but my understanding is that he took residence here before I—ah—went away. I do not think that Alderney is the man, Mr. Dawlish."

"Why should you?" countered Dawlish.

"I have wondered whether the police thought so," said Fripp.

"Very smart of you," murmured Dawlish.

"No, not smart at all," said Fripp, earnestly, "I would have been very slow had I failed to do so. Well, Mr. Dawlish, I was interested in the identity of this particular fence. Is that surprising?"

"I suppose not," said Dawlish.

"What is more, while in prison I learned—somewhat vaguely, I fear—of great plans being made for operations on a very wide scale. Few criminals are fools. They know that conditions today are as favourable as ever they are likely to be for successful—ah—activities. There were one or two jewel thieves of extreme ability with me, and I gathered that there would be a series of hold-ups—such as we had the other night near here— and country house burglaries. It was felt that the crime wave in London would force Scotland Yard to take defensive measures which would make London a difficult field of operations, so it was agreed to transfer activities to a wider sphere."

"Most enterprising," said Dawlish.

"They are enterprising," Fripp assured him. "While I do not approve, I admit I admire the way they work and plan." His eyes gleamed innocently. "Are their ways so different from unscrupulous business men, I wonder."

"A fair amount of difference," Dawlish said.

"Perhaps you are right, Mr. Dawlish. I have little time for business men myself. I spent my five years inside prison walls owing to their activities." His smile was soft and genial. "I bear no grievance, nor do I thirst for revenge, though I know that you are unlikely to believe me when I say that I was imprisoned for a crime which I did not commit."

"Without knowing the circumstances I can form no opinion," Dawlish said punctiliously.

"I will give you the details, a little later, if it would interest you," Fripp promised. "Now, sir, to the point. It had come to my knowledge that a fence of some power lived in this district. I admit I was curious. I decided therefore that I would choose this time rather than any other, to revisit the home of my youth."

"Just as an observer?" asked Dawlish, sceptically.

Fripp shrugged his shoulders. "Isn't curiosity enough? After all, the fence is presumably a man with a good reputation, one who was, perhaps, at the ball the other evening, someone who is so respected, someone who might even be a close personal friend of the Chief Constable. Yes, I was interested! And I wanted to make observations. I have been in the district for several weeks. After spending five years behind prison bars expiating a crime I didn't commit, such freedom is very dear to me."

Dawlish said slowly: "And the observations you wanted to make—were they successful?"

"They might be called so," Fripp said genially. "I visited Alderney House, for instance, because I recognised one of the staff as a Parkmoor acquaintance of mine. I wondered what he was doing there, and how he had obtained employment in such a household. So, I went to make enquiries about the Alderneys. I gathered that the staff at the house holds its master and mistress in high regard. Nevertheless, a habitual criminal is living there, Mr. Dawlish. Does that interest you?"

"It does indeed," said Dawlish.

"In fact"—Fripp's voice sank to a childlike whisper of astonishment—"there are three habitual criminals in that house!"

Dawlish leaned forward.

"I saw them there on the evening of the fire," Fripp continued. "I was very interested indeed. They did exactly as Alderney told them, yet it would not really surprise me if they were responsible for the fire. Nor would it surprise me if they were deliberately slow in fighting it."

"And your reasons for such a suspicion?"

"Perhaps, because it was the only way of finding out what was in the vaults," said Fripp. "Do you know whether Sir Brian kept many valuables in them?"

Dawlish shook his head.

"I suppose it is unlikely that he would tell you," said Fripp. "I am quite sure that the men are not reformed, and that they are there, either with or without his consent, for a nefarious purpose. Do you know anything about his more distant past?"

"Very little."

"Dear me," said Fripp, "you don't know much, Mr. Dawlish, do you? The impression I received from those—ah—friends of yours in Parkmoor was that you knew a great many things, and that you were a wiz—that was the word often used—a wiz at discovering information. But perhaps you are taking only a tepid interest in what is going on around you."

Dawlish smiled. "Possibly."

"On the other hand, perhaps you are not prepared to tell

me how much you know. That would not really be surprising. But I have been frank with you, Mr. Dawlish. I have told you everything that I think might be useful. And I may be able to do more, if you will tell me what you want to know."

"Why do you think you were attacked?" Dawlish asked evenly.

Fripp's eyebrows rose dramatically.

"*Surely* you can guess that."

"You were recognised, and there was concern lest you, too, recognised the servants at the house?"

"Very ably put," said Fripp. "They are also not unaware of your reputation. It follows quite logically therefore, that in order to make sure that I could not tell you the truth about them, they endeavoured to kill me. They were wise enough, however, to employ strangers. I recognised neither of my assailants. They were certainly not men whom I met in prison. And that," added Fripp, very gently, "leads me to a matter of great importance, my gratitude to you and your friends. But for your prompt interference, I would not be alive today." He touched his neck, gingerly.

"It was the police who gave the alarm," said Dawlish.

"But it was you who acted," said Fripp. "I do want to assure you that I am really deeply grateful, Mr. Dawlish. I am entirely at your service from now on. If there is anything I can do to help, please tell me."

"Thank you," said Dawlish, formally.

Fripp looked at him with a somewhat puzzled frown. Dawlish's expression was withdrawn and wooden; so also was Beresford's, at whom the little man glanced quickly. There was silence in the room for some time. Dawlish did not move or relax, and the little man sat still.

At last he broke the silence.

"I do hope you are not doubting what I have told you," he murmured.

"No, I don't doubt you," said Dawlish, abruptly, "but I think you might be able to tell me a lot more."

"Such as?"

"Does your aunt know that you're here?"

"She does not! And I do not want her to be distressed, Mr. Dawlish. It was a great blow to her when I was sent to prison. Pride is more painfully hurt than love."

"She cut you off with a shilling?"

"*Without* a shilling," corrected Fripp.

"But, coming here, you must have known there was a risk that she would know you're in the neighbourhood."

Fripp smiled.

"My aunt probably knows every person of consequence within a fifty mile radius, but *not* the rogues and vagabonds. No, there's little danger that she will come to know that I am in the district, Mr. Dawlish."

"I see. What about the police?"

"Once they know who I am, they will doubtless hold me on suspicion," said Fripp, "unless, of course, you, who work so independently of the police at times, might withhold this information?" His voice was casual, but there was intensity behind it.

"It is possible, but I cannot promise," said Dawlish.

"You're very good!"

"Meanwhile, you'll be well advised to stay here, and if you take sudden leave, the police will be after you before you've gone a mile."

"I am only too content to stay," Fripp assured him. "Do apologise to your charming wife, for any trouble I may be causing."

Dawlish left the little man still murmuring apologies and benedictions, and went downstairs with Beresford. He was limping badly. Sinking down into an armchair, he gave a sigh of relief. They sat smoking in silence for a long time, while

Dawlish let his thoughts roam. One idea he felt sure that he and Beresford had in common: the man upstairs had not told them all the truth, but what he had told them shone a new light on Alderney. Like Leven, they had assumed, from the visits from known criminals, that Alderney was deliberately working with them. This new light suggested that he was being blackmailed into taking a certain course of action.

Dawlish pondered over Alderney's reaction to the fire.

He felt more than ever certain that it was essential to see Alderney, and make a further effort to get the whole truth from him. Above all things, Dawlish wanted to know who the girl victim of the fire really was.

They talked in desultory fashion for the better part of an hour. Then Felicity came in from the garden, excited with the news she was about to impart.

"Alderney's on his way here," she announced. "I've just seen the Rolls."

Chapter 10

CAUSE FOR ALARM

Alderney jumped out of his car almost before it stopped. He was frowning; almost, in fact, scowling.

Chloe opened the door as he reached the porch.

"Good-morning, sir."

"Ask Mr. Dawlish to see me, at once," said Alderney.

"I'll find out whether he is in, sir," said Chloe, mildly.

"I must see him—*at once*," said Alderney, sharply.

Chloe said: "Very good, sir," and walked quickly to the sitting-room.

"Are we in this?" whispered Beresford.

Dawlish gave a quick nod, which passed on to Chloe. He was as anxious to see Alderney as the man was to see him.

Alderney strode in, nodded curtly to Felicity and Beresford, and stood in front of Dawlish, staring down; glaring down. Something was obviously seriously amiss.

"Where is my wife?" snapped Alderney.

Dawlish blinked. "What's that?"

Alderney raised clenched fists.

"Dawlish, I will not tolerate interference in my affairs.

I will not be fobbed off with evasive answers. Where's my wife?"

"I haven't the faintest idea," drawled Dawlish.

Alderney swung round on Felicity.

"Mrs. Dawlish, I warn you that I will not be trifled with. Your husband has a reputation for being stubborn, but unless he tells me the truth, I will—I will put an end to his career at this house." The climax was weak, yet the man's manner saved it from being ludicrous. "Presumably you have influence with him."

Dawlish stretched out a hand and touched the man's arm.

"Sit down, Alderney. Ted, get some drinks, will you? Now, what's all this about your wife?"

Alderney stood quite still.

"I've told you that I will not be satisfied with evasive answers."

"My dear chap, *I* don't know anything about your wife," Dawlish said. "If anything's wrong and I can help, I will, gladly."

"My wife came to see you yesterday evening, and has not returned."

There was a pregnant pause.

"Damn you, answer me!" roared Alderney, and moved forward, as if prepared to strike. Ted went out of the room unconcernedly, as if this were an everyday occurrence. Felicity tightened her hands in her lap, but did not move.

"You sent for her, and—"

"Let's get this straight," said Dawlish levelly. "First, I didn't send for her; second, the last time any of us saw her was when she came to ask my wife to persuade me to help."

"All right!" said Alderney, "have it your own way."

He looked round, his eyes flashing. Espying the telephone, he strode towards it. Dawlish did not even turn his head to watch him, but Felicity saw his strained eyes, the pallor of his cheeks as he seized the receiver. She exchanged startled glances with Dawlish.

"Get me the Haslemere police station."

Alderney waited, standing quite still. Ted came in with a tray of bottles and glasses. He began to pour out, still behaving as if this were the most ordinary thing in the world.

"Inspector Leven, please," said Alderney, abruptly. "This is Sir Brian Alderney."

There was a short pause.

"Ah, hallo Leven," said Alderney in a clipped voice. "I have reason to believe that Dawlish has kidnapped my wife. I am at his house now. Will you come at once . . . No, it can't wait! . . . Yes, I will stay here." He banged the receiver down and turned.

"What'll you have?" asked Beresford.

Alderney ignored him.

"Dawlish, I am not fooling, and—"

"Oh, please don't prance about like an Edwardian dancing master, it's so confusing," suggested Dawlish. "Sit down and have a drink." He stretched out his hand for a whisky and soda. "Do believe me when I say that if I knew anything about your wife, I'd tell you."

"You must believe that," Felicity said, quietly.

"But you were right to send for the police. If she's missing they should know at once."

Alderney looked distractedly from one to the other of them.

"When did you last see her?" asked Dawlish.

"Yesterday afternoon."

"Did you know she was supposed to be coming here?"

"Not before she left." Alderney picked up a whisky and soda and drained the glass at a gulp. Then he sat on the arm of a chair opposite Dawlish. The colour slowly returned to his face. "Are you telling me the truth, Dawlish?"

"Of course I am. Someone may have used my name to get her away from *Akers*, but I know nothing about it. Do you say she's been missing all night?"

"Yes," said Alderney, slowly. "I felt sure—Dawlish, what game are you playing?"

"At the moment, I'm nursing an injured knee," Dawlish said.

Alderney looked at his leg as if he had noticed nothing amiss before.

"You know what I mean," he said.

Dawlish sipped his drink.

"And you should know what I do. You asked me to help in this amazing affair, and I turned you down. Isn't that enough? I'm a peace-loving apple-grower with no liking for violence. I gave shelter to a tramp, and got a smashed knee for my pains, but I'm still peace-loving." He spoke in a drawling voice, watching Alderney all the time. "Do you seriously think that anything has happened to your wife?"

"She wouldn't disappear of her own accord," said Alderney. "She is missing." He sat quite still for what seemed a long time, and then he asked abruptly: "All right, Dawlish—if I take your word for it, will you help me to find her?"

"If I can."

Alderney got up, and walked to the window. He was a badly worried man, trying hard to regain his composure. He stood there for some time, while the others sat in silence, then turned slowly.

"It begins to look as if an apology is overdue," he said. "I know something of your reputation, Dawlish, and I know you use methods peculiarly your own. I thought you wanted to get some information out of me, and were trying this way to force me to talk."

"How Machiavellian can you get?" murmured Dawlish. "However, I do want information from you. Before I offer to lend a hand, I'll have to know the whole story. But before we go into that, what will you say to Leven when he comes?"

Alderney hesitated. "Will Leven believe me if I tell him that I was mistaken about the kidnapper?"

"He'll have to," said Dawlish.

"Have I made difficulties for you?"

Dawlish laughed. "The police have all kinds of wild theories about what I do and what I don't do. They're like you—prepared to believe anything. Four men are in or near the grounds now, a measure of their trust."

"I see," said Alderney, slowly.

Leven arrived with his usual promptness. He was sporting a new suit, and looked very young. Dawlish, quick to observe, thought that something had pleased the Inspector; he had an air of confidence and satisfaction as he came into the room, a great change from his harassed and worried countenance of the past few days.

"Now what's all this?" he asked.

Alderney's manner had also changed; Dawlish marvelled at his ability to adapt himself to any given circumstances. Now and again he lost control, but it always came back fairly quickly.

"I seem to have made a fool of myself, Inspector."

Leven raised his eyebrows.

"Indeed?" The word gave the impression that he was not at all surprised.

"Yes. My wife left, as I understood, to see Mr. Dawlish yesterday evening. She has not returned. I blamed Dawlish, but—"

"Not guilty," said Dawlish, "but the situation is worrying, Inspector." He spoke rather formally, hoping that Leven would understand why; Leven obviously did. "Lady Alderney ought to have been back by now."

"Do you mean you haven't heard from her since last night?" asked Leven, startled.

"That is so," said Alderney. "Dawlish has convinced me that he knows nothing about it. It's just possible that she has gone off of her own accord—"

"Has she done that before?" asked Leven.

"I have known her go away for a day or two," said Alderney, "but never without sending me a message."

"Do you want to report her formally as missing?"

"Certainly I do."

Leven waited for no further information, but went to the telephone and called his office. He gave instructions for an official watch to be kept for Lady Alderney and for her description to be circulated throughout the Home Counties, promising that photographs would soon be forthcoming.

"Now let me hear about it," he said.

The story was simple. Alderney had been out the previous evening, calling on Colonel Maitland, the Courtlands and Lady Fripp, to discuss the jewel robberies and their hope that Dawlish would take part in the investigations. On his return, he learned that his wife had left *Akers* in her own Daimler. When she did not return after an hour, he made further inquiries and was told that Dawlish had telephoned to ask her to call and see him.

"That's all," he said.

Leven raised his eyebrows.

"Not quite all, Sir Brian. Weren't you alarmed when she did not return last night?"

"I didn't know," said Alderney.

Leven stared.

"I had a severe headache," Alderney told him. "That's not unusual, and when attacked in this way I retire to bed early, and sleep late. I didn't realise that my wife was still away until half an hour before I came over here."

"I see," said Leven, as if he neither saw nor believed. "Have you raised an alarm at the house?"

"No. I took it for granted that it was a stunt of Dawlish's."

"Why?"

Alderney shrugged. "You should know that he has a reputation for that kind of thing," he said.

Leven hesitated, and then turned to Dawlish. There was just the right touch of coldness in his manner as he asked:

"*Do* you know anything about this, Mr. Dawlish?"

"Only that my name was most certainly misappropriated," he said.

"Humph. Very well, Sir Brian—I assure you that we shall do everything we can to find her, although I hope—" he paused.

"Go on."

"I hope it isn't a storm in a tea-cup," Leven said. "We have a great deal to do, and you seem to admit the possibility that she has gone off of her own accord."

"I don't think she would have said that Dawlish had called her, if she didn't think he had," said Alderney, slowly.

"Right!" said Leven. He crossed to the door. "There's nothing else at all that you can tell me?"

"Nothing."

"You'll let us know if you hear from her," said Leven, and went out, nodding to the men, smiling slightly at Felicity. His car went down the drive, and was out of sight before any of the others spoke. Dawlish was reflecting that Leven would consider Alderney's manner strange, to say the least of it. Until he remembered how the man had behaved when he had first arrived, it was difficult to believe that he was seriously troubled about his wife's disappearance. He watched him steadily. The anxiety was there; it showed in the man's eyes, although a casual observer might have failed to notice it.

Then Alderney did a strange thing:

"I shall be even further in their black books now." He laughed, without much humour.

"I know that I'm suspect Number 1, and if that weren't almost tragic, it would be funny. You're sold on the same idea, Dawlish, aren't you? You think I know something about the hold-ups and the jewel-robberies."

There was a long pause; and then Dawlish said:

"Yes, I do."

Alderney raised his eyebrows. "Well, that's frank enough."

"There isn't time for verbal skirmishes," said Dawlish. "I know another thing, Alderney. You're in a spot, and your wife may be in a worse one."

"How much *do* you know?"

"That among your staff you've several habitual criminals," said Dawlish. "I don't think the police are aware of that yet. That you get visits from others—the police do know that. That you haven't told us the truth about the fire, or about Mary Keen. And that if you go on like this, you'll be in serious trouble before it's over." He took out cigarettes, and offered them. "Are you being blackmailed?" he asked.

After a long pause, Alderney said slowly:

"Yes, Dawlish, I am. I thought that I was strong enough to fight it, but I'm beginning to wonder. I've played a dangerous game, I've asked for trouble, but now—" he shrugged his shoulders. "I don't think I can cope on my own. I'm gradually reaching a frame of mind where I don't greatly care, provided my wife is all right. That's beginning to worry me seriously. It's only now dawning on me that these other people are getting really dangerous."

"Which puts her in a nasty spot," Dawlish repeated.

"Yes and no," said Alderney. "I've enough on them to make sure that they don't let her come to any harm. And I—"

He stopped as the telephone bell rang. Felicity jumped up to answer it. The noise had put Alderney off his stroke, and the intervening pause gave Dawlish time to study him. Beneath that acquired habit of confidence and authority, he could see that the man was seriously worried.

"Yes, he's here," said Felicity, with a tone of surprise in her voice. "Hold on, please." She turned. "It's a London call for you, Sir Brian."

Alderney said: "But no one knows I'm here." He crossed the room and took the telephone, nevertheless. "Alderney speaking . . . Yes . . ." he drew in his breath sharply, and then went on in a softer voice: "Janice, my dear . . ."

Every eye was turned towards him, every moment was stilled.

"I see," said Alderney, at last. "Good-bye, darling." He replaced the receiver slowly, looked at the others, then crossed to the window.

He began to speak, slowly.

"I am afraid that has made some difference," he said. The words seemed to be dragged from his lips. "I have made a complete fool of myself." He turned and looked at Dawlish, with his lips twisted. "She has—"

He started.

From somewhere outside, there came the sharp crack of a shot.

Alderney staggered and put out a hand to save himself as Felicity plunged forward to save him from falling. She failed. Dawlish got up with difficulty, staring at the man, seeing the blood on his temple.

The blast of a police whistle shrilled through the room.

Chapter 11

DAWLISH IS FRUSTRATED

Felicity went down on one knee beside Alderney, Dawlish hobbled towards him, and Beresford swung away from the window and made for the door. Dawlish longed to follow him, but Ted, even with his artificial leg, could have given him a long start. Men were on the move outside; it was a good thing that Leven had made sure that police were stationed about the house. Dawlish saw two uniformed figures run past the window, one of them pointing towards a distant field.

"How is he?" Dawlish asked, gruffly.

"I don't think it's much," said Felicity. "Give me your handkerchief."

She pressed it gently against the wound. Dawlish got down on one knee with difficulty. He saw that the shot, breaking no bones, had left only a shallow furrow. Alderney was stunned, but not seriously hurt.

"I'll get some water," Felicity said.

Dawlish felt helpless, angry and frustrated. He ought to be out there, joining in the chase. He looked at Alderney's set face; yes, he was a good-looking beggar. Beneath that façade of confidence, Dawlish thought that he was at his wits' end. His behaviour that morning had seemed out of character, but was understandable if he were in dire straits.

Felicity came back with a bowl of water, a towel and first-aid equipment. Dawlish helped her to get Alderney onto a settee, then hobbled to the wall.

The bullet had buried itself deep in the plaster. The most nervewracking feature of this affair was the daring which the criminals were showing; and their seemingly endless resources.

He looked back at Alderney, whose eyes were flickering open.

"He'll be all right," said Felicity.

Dawlish went to the window, the feeling of frustration strong within him. The men were out of sight. He might have outdistanced them all, with two sound legs. As it was, he knew that the only way to get his leg back to normal was to rest it; he ought to stay in bed for two or three days.

He would have to do that.

Felicity murmured: "Stay with him, while I make him a cup of tea."

Alderney stared blankly at Dawlish.

"You'll be all right in half an hour," Dawlish assured him. "How's the head feeling now?"

Alderney's hand strayed to his temple, touched the dressing, and stayed there. "What happened?"

"Someone took a pot-shot at you," said Dawlish.

He was puzzled by the man's attitude, but put it down to slight concussion. Many a man had received a more serious wound than that and not lost consciousness; there seemed no other explanation for the dazed look in his eyes.

Alderney drew a long, slow breath.

"Who are you?" he asked.

Dawlish frowned. "Now, come—"

"Who are you?" Alderney's voice sharpened.

"Dawlish," said Dawlish.

"Where am I?"

Dawlish stood staring down at the man. This was fantastic. Could a mild concussion cause a lapse of memory like this? Would it come so quickly?

"Answer me!" snapped Alderney.

"Now don't work yourself up," Dawlish pleaded. "You're at my house—the house of a friend. You've had a knock on the head, but it isn't serious. You were just speaking to your wife."

Alderney started. "My *wife?*"

"Yes, she—"

"Don't be absurd," said Alderney. "I'm not married."

By the middle of the afternoon, two doctors from Haslemere had seen Alderney, and agreed in their opinion; the blow had been severe enough to make him lose his memory. It was only temporary, they said, and advised that he should be sent home to bed, and allowed to rest undisturbed for a few days. Memory might return at any moment; the lapse might not last for more than a few hours. With that, Dawlish and Leven, who had come with them, had to be satisfied. The doctors prepared to leave, suggesting that they should get in touch with a day and a night nurse—in his condition, it would not be wise to leave him unattended.

"We'll see to it," Dawlish promised.

"I think we had better—" one of them began.

Dawlish smiled. "Leave it to us, please."

When they had gone, silently, and a little disapproving, Dawlish looked at Leven and took out his cigarettes.

"Why didn't you want them to arrange for the nurses?" said Leven.

"My dear chap! That's your job. Police nurses, I think—you can find a couple, can't you? And Alderney shouldn't go to his own house. The staff can't be trusted. Any objection to him staying here?"

"I suppose not," said Leven, slowly. "You think he might ramble a bit?" He smiled. "I hadn't thought of that, but it would be useful if he did."

"The ravings of a man in delirium can't be taken as evidence," said Dawlish, mechanically, and then laughed. "Leven, we've been very nicely bluffed."

Leven stared.

"Oh, *I'm* not raving," Dawlish assured him, "it's all very neatly done. Alderney was on the point of telling me what was troubling him, when his wife telephoned—"

"In person?"

"I gather so. And whatever she said, it made him change his mind. Then came the shooting. I think he was knocked out, but I don't think he was unconscious for as long as he pretended to be. I think he was very much on the alert. His mind works quickly, you know. He knew that he would be pestered with questions, he had reason not to talk, and so he decided to pretend that he had lost his memory."

"Now, look here," protested Leven, "two doctors—"

"Any doctor will tell you that it's almost impossible to be sure that a man has lost his memory," said Dawlish. "It's a difficult thing to diagnose. You've got to rely on the truth of what your patient tells you." He laughed again. "His words when he came round didn't ring true. And he appears—or pretends now—to have forgotten everything, but he remembered to tell me that he wasn't married. A wrong move. For a few minutes, he really took me in. What could be a better way of dodging questions than a sudden attack of amnesia?"

Leven said slowly:

"We can put him through some pretty severe tests."

"I think we'd be wise to leave him for the time being," said Dawlish. "Let him think he's getting away with it. When he realises that he's being kept here, it won't please him, but as he claims not to know who he is, he can't very well grumble if he's not sent to his own home."

Leven laughed. "Caught in his own trap, so to speak."

"There isn't a great deal you can tackle him about," said Dawlish. "Little's known against him." He had told Leven part of Fripp's story. "It's not a crime to employ criminals—in fact in some quarters it's regarded as philanthropy!"

"It means you'll be having a pretty full house," Leven observed, after a pause.

"We'll manage," said Dawlish. "There's no news of Lady Alderney, I suppose?"

"No. Doesn't the telephone call suggest that she's free enough?"

"Not necessarily. Anyhow, he made a formal request for help, and you've an excuse to search for her. You can look over his house, too. If I were you, I'd do just that," said Dawlish. "You might be able to find Lady Alderney, although I'm not sanguine. This business gets deeper with every new twist," he added, "and more confusing. No trace of this morning's sharpshooter, I suppose?"

"He got away on a motor-cycle," Leven said gloomily.

"What about the robberies? Any more?"

"None at all—we haven't had such a long break for weeks."

"They're preparing for a big show, probably," said Dawlish, and looked at his leg. "I hope they take a long time to prepare!" He smiled, and changed the subject. "What were you looking so pleased about when you came in this morning?"

"Oh, that," said Leven, a little too casually. "I've just become Chief Inspector."

"Congratulations!" cried Dawlish heartily, "I'm delighted."

There followed a week in which little or nothing happened. At long last the police had got a complete set of Alderney's fingerprints, but they said nothing to Dawlish afterwards, so presumably they drew a blank.

He lay in bed upstairs, unprotesting, with a police-nurse on duty all the time—a woman by day, a man at night. He asked for nothing, and did not once let slip a clue which might suggest that he was hoaxing them. He made no inquiries about his wife or friends, and he did not respond by a flicker of an eyelid when he was addressed by his own name. By the end of the fifth day, only Dawlish clung to the theory that he was pretending. Even Felicity felt quite sure that it was a genuine case of loss of memory; and the doctors had no doubt at all.

Fripp made himself most useful.

He did odd jobs about the house and the garden with eager cheerfulness, spending much of the day perched among the trees, picking apples, while Beresford or Felicity stayed below, packing them into baskets.

There was no news of Lady Alderney.

Leven put a sergeant and two policemen on duty at *Akers*. After consultation with Dawlish and Trivett, it had been decided that the police should not disclose the fact that they knew the identity of three members of the staff, but the men were watched, and there was no difficulty in getting impressions from their fingers. Fripp was right; they were habitual criminals, and at some time or other in their careers they had touched jewellery.

No one visited *Akers*.

'Mary Keen' could not be traced.

Felicity, at Dawlish's suggestion, mixed as freely with the people from the surrounding district as she could, and brought back reports every day. The loss of jewels was still a sore point with everyone. There was a lot of sympathy for Alderney and Dawlish. Most of the people thought that they had suffered in trying to be helpful, and from day to day gifts of fruit, cream and flowers were delivered to *Four Ways* for the invalids.

On the second day of his enforced inactivity, Dawlish received from Trivett a long account of Fripp's trial and sentence. He had actually been given six years hard labour for a crime it was difficult to associate with him—embezzlement with violence! He had been a solicitor with a small practice in a London suburb, and had embezzled some five thousand pounds of his clients' money. One of them, on discovering that money was missing, had tackled him, and Fripp had become violent. The victim had been in hospital for three weeks as a result of a head wound caused by an ebony ruler. They had been alone in the office at the time. Fripp had admitted losing his temper and striking the man, but had not admitted embezzlement; his books, however, were in a hopeless state of confusion, and the evidence had been so strong that there had been little doubt of the verdict.

Dawlish wondered if it could be true that he had been victimised. The more he thought of Fripp's case, the more curious he became about the 'victim' of his attack. Trivett, showing little interest, had promised to find out what the man, a certain Roland Mortimer, was now doing. According to the court records, he had been a 'General Merchant' at the time of the attack; but 'General Merchant', as Dawlish pointed out, could cover a multitude of crimes.

All these things, chafing at his inactivity, Dawlish turned over in his mind.

Soon, the nine days having run their course, the hold-ups ceased to be the main topic of conversation in the district.

The police made no further arrests, and failed to glean any more information from the men who were in custody. All of them had been before the magistrates twice, and had been remanded for trial by jury.

On the tenth day, when Dawlish was moving about with much greater freedom, Beresford, opening his letters at breakfast, pulled a face.

"Bad news?" asked Felicity, lightly; one did not associate Ted Beresford with bad news.

"It's not too good, Joan's down with 'flu." He looked troubled. "You know, Pat, I ought to get back to London. I hoped that things would break by now, but this do-nothing period might last for weeks yet—is there anything I could do in Town?"

"That's a thought," said Dawlish, slowly. "Trivett isn't too set on checking Roland Mortimer." He took an envelope from his pocket. "The last heard of Mortimer was at the latter stage of the war, when he was travelling representative for a firm of warehousemen. We don't know what he's doing now. Have a word with Tim, and see what you can find out between you, will you?"

"I certainly will," promised Ted, relieved that circumstances would not thrust him entirely out of the fray. Standing at the window, from which they seemed to have seen so much of this affair, Dawlish and Felicity watched his car retreating down the drive.

"Well, we're almost back where we started from," Dawlish observed, as the car finally disappeared.

"We're further back," Felicity declared, "if you take into account the fanciful dreams you will insist on weaving about poor Alderney."

"Not more fanciful than the decision of the females of the household to call little Fripp—soberly baptised Robert John—by the frivolous name of 'Percy'."

"He likes it."

"Darling child—" murmured Dawlish. "Hallo! another visitor. Whose antiquated chariot is that, now?" An old Austin was coming up the drive, with a chauffeur, a big, well-built fellow Who looked out of place in his uniform and peaked hat, at the wheel. Dawlish's eyes brightened. "It's Lady Fripp, isn't it?"

"It's certainly her car."

"Where's nephew Percy?" asked Dawlish.

A faint whistling sound was coming from the side of the house, where Fripp was busy in a small greenhouse, dusting tomato plants with soot, which he declared gave them a better flavour. The car drew up. Fripp, who was always curious, loomed short-sightedly into view, flourishing a pair of secateurs in his hand; for he had the right idea of always appearing to be busy.

Lady Fripp, dressed in rustling black relieved by white trimming, was being helped from the car by her chauffeur.

Percy swung round.

Lady Fripp stared at him for what seemed a long time, and then made her stately way towards the house. She was a tall woman, with an angular figure, and although her black dress rustled, it was modish, like the small hat she wore on her magnificent grey hair.

Percy disappeared, with the speed of a frightened rabbit.

"He seems pretty sure she will recognise him," Felicity said, slowly.

"In spite of his earlier confidence," said Dawlish. "My sweet, there's more in Percy Fripp than meets the eye. Are you going to meet the old dame?"

"Chloe's in the village, so I'll have to," said Felicity. "I expect she's come to inquire after you, so look ill."

Dawlish, the picture of health, grimaced at her and sank down into what he imagined to be an invalid's posture.

A face appeared at the window.

Dawlish started. The door began to open, and Lady Fripp's voice grew louder.

"*Mr. Dawlish*," whispered Fripp from the window, "It's urgent, I-must-have-a-word with-you."

"Oh, yes, he's *much* better," Felicity was saying.

"*Urgent!*" mouthed Percy, pushing the window up, in an invitation for Dawlish to climb out.

The door was wider open now. Dawlish was behind it. He stepped over the window sill, and disappeared from the room.

"Darling," said Felicity, "Lady Fripp has—"

She broke off abruply; Dawlish could imagine her feelings.

Percy had moved from the house, and was beckoning him. Dawlish was aware of two things at once. The chauffeur could just see him, though not Percy, and must be wondering what he was doing; and, a cause for rejoicing, he had carried his full weight on his right let without a twinge of pain.

Fripp disappeared into the greenhouse.

"Now, what is it?" demanded Dawlish, ducking to get beneath the lintel.

He was astonished at the pallor of the man's face. Percy had grown plump, but now he sagged; and he was trembling. Dawlish expected to be begged to say nothing to Lady Fripp. He was astonished that the man should be so affected by the nearness of his aunt; he had never suggested that he was in any way troubled by her.

Fripp's lips were dry, and he tried twice to speak before he was successful. "That—man, Mr. Dawlish."

"Man?" Dawlish's voice sharpened.

"The chauffeur. He—what is he doing with my aunt? What is he doing here? He is the man responsible for my imprisonment, the man I told you about—Roland Mortimer. I can't be mistaken, I shall remember him until my dying day!"

Chapter 12

MY LADY'S MEMORY

"I have no doubt at all that the man is Roland Mortimer," Fripp insisted, "the man who deliberately and with such dreadful malice sent me to jail. Why is he with my aunt?"

"We'll find out," said Dawlish, reassuringly.

He had always thought that there was much of the child in Percy Fripp. Now, as he looked at the little man, who had lost his colour and was actually trembling, he wondered if five years in jail had weakened his mind. It was surprising that the appearance of Mortimer had so affected him; it was natural, doubtless, that he should be shocked, but hardly natural that he should be so pale and upset.

"We must find out," muttered Percy, "but—I don't want to see him, Mr. Dawlish. I—I can't trust myself with that man."

Dawlish looked at him sharply, but did not press the question.

"Go and stroll through the orchard," he advised. "Mortimer won't be here very long."

"You *will* make inquiries, won't you?"

"Urgent inquiries," Dawlish assured him.

He restrained himself from patting Percy on the head, touched his shoulder instead, and then went out. He saw that the chauffeur had left the car and was looking at the flower beds which lay near the greenhouse. Dawlish did not know whether he was actually trying to see Percy Fripp, or whether he was bored and wanted to stretch his legs.

It was Percy's reactions which interested him.

The little man was standing with a hand on the greenhouse door, and staring towards the chauffeur. There was a new light in his eyes, one Dawlish had never seen before, or dreamed any man had the power to ignite in the soul or body of Percy Fripp. It was one of pure hatred.

"We'll have to be very, very careful," Dawlish thought.

As he strode towards the sitting-room, he wondered whether Fripp had learned that Mortimer was in the district and had come to seek him out, but dismissed it as being unlikely. The door was ajar, and he thrust it open, going forward to greet Lady Fripp as if she were a long-lost friend. "How nice to see you! And a thousand thanks for the fruit and cream." He took both her hands, releasing them with flattering reluctance. "These are hard days," he said, "one of the policemen outside was making weird signals, and I had to go out and see what he wanted. The ass thought he'd seen a man prowling near. I believe it was his shadow, but with so much happening, I had to take him seriously. I know you understand." He offered her a cigarette, and to his surprise, she took it.

"Thank you, Major Dawlish. I am very glad to see you looking so well. From all accounts, I thought you were at death's door."

"Not this time."

The gleam in Lady Fripp's eyes, which the discerning Beresford had seen when he had first met her, pleased Dawlish.

"Evidently rumour exaggerated. Are you fully recovered?"

"Oh, yes." Dawlish smiled, then frowned. "I wish we could say the same of poor Alderney."

"How ill is Sir Brian?" asked Lady Fripp.

"In himself, he's all right. It's the question of his past," said Dawlish, solemnly.

Lady Fripp's eyes lost their twinkle; in a flash they became frosty, almost suspicious.

"Past?"

"Well, yes, he seems to have forgotten it, and we're trying to build it up for him. If you could help—"

"Major Dawlish," said Lady Fripp, ominously.

"Yes?" He waited, with a hopeful smile.

"It would save you a lot of bother, and me a certain amount of irritation, if I told you at once that I am not a fool."

Dawlish looked aghast. "My dear Lady Fripp!"

"My dear man—" she drummed her pointed, delicately manicured fingers impatiently on a nearby table, "you forget, I think, that my late husband was one of the finest Counsels in the country. I am not unversed in the ways of cross-examination."

As Dawlish smiled, the frostiness faded from Lady Fripp's eyes, and the twinkle returned.

"Major Dawlish, I came here to see you with a very definite purpose, and I want you to treat me seriously. What *is* the matter with Sir Brian Alderney?"

Dawlish hesitated for some time, and then said slowly:

"He says that he has lost his memory."

"*Says?*"

"Convincingly," murmured Dawlish.

"Pat—" began Felicity.

"Hush, my dear," said Lady Fripp. "I have spoken to the

doctors, Major Dawlish, and they are in no doubt at all about the amnesia. It is not unusual. Why do you doubt it?"

"It came at such a convenient time," said Dawlish.

"Ahhh," sighed Lady Fripp, and settled back in her chair. "I was wondering when *someone* would realise that. Is he still confined to his room?"

"Yes."

"Does he show no desire to leave it, to walk about the grounds?"

"None."

"I see. Yes, it is a most curious business. I am very interested in Sir Brian Alderney," she added, and then gave a hard little laugh. "I know he is extremely popular, but—and I speak deliberately— he has *bought* much of his popularity, and his wife has bought the rest."

Dawlish murmured: "This is straight talk."

"Yes," said Lady Fripp, "and there are times when straight talk is necessary. This, I think, is one of them. I know that you have not allowed the truth to be generally known, but I can read between the lines—if you weren't in considerable danger, you would not allow four policemen to be on duty in the grounds of your house. If the police were not extremely interested in Brian Alderney, they would not have sent policemen to his house while he is staying under your roof. Since the night of the ball, the district has become the centre of violence and crime, Major Dawlish, and you have been deeply involved in it. From the beginning, Brian Alderney *wanted* you involved. You realised that, I have no doubt."

"Yes," murmured Dawlish.

"At no time have I classified you as a fool," declared Lady Fripp, "but your behaviour, at times, does puzzle me. There are several things I would like to know. Among them—why do you allow my nephew to live here, Major Dawlish?"

She could not have created greater effect had she produced a rabbit from her cuff. Felicity gasped. Dawlish's face dropped ludicrously. He was taken completely off his guard, his expression was a tacit admission that she had discovered the truth. As he looked at the triumphant smile on her lips, he thought ruefully that it had taken one old woman in her seventies to discompose him completely.

"Well," she asked. "Why do you?"

Dawlish got up, and moved about the room. He did not know how best to answer, but find an answer he must.

"The poor chap's in need of a roof over his head," he said at last.

"Paugh! The man's a rogue!"

"I know he blotted the Fripp escutcheon pretty badly," said Dawlish, "but aren't you a little hard?"

"Not a shade harder than he deserves," snapped Lady Fripp. She had nearly lost her temper; Dawlish had succeeded in finding the one answer which would discompose her. She looked angry. "He is a plausible scoundrel, Major Dawlish, and I thought you had sufficient common sense to realise it." She sat erect. "Is it not true that you discovered who he was and kept him here in the hope that you would be able to persuade me, through him, to talk freely?"

Dawlish's eyes crinkled at the corners.

"Partly," he said.

"I thought so." She was still angry, and Dawlish began to wonder whether he would have been wiser to allow her to enjoy her triumph to the full. It looked as if he had made a tactical mistake at a time when disclosures of considerable importance might have been forthcoming. But he retained an amiable smile, and watched her closely.

"After all," said Dawlish, "you encouraged Alderney to appeal for my help, didn't you?"

"So would any sensible woman," snapped Lady Fripp. "Why didn't you come to me and ask me straight out what you wanted to know?"

"But I don't yet know what I want to know, or what you might be able to tell me."

"I *see*," said Lady Fripp, heavily. "Then I will tell you all I can and you can make the best use of it that *you* can. I am an old woman with a most retentive memory. I can remember many things which the police forget—or have never known. I can remember, for instance, when Alderney was sent to prison for manslaughter. Had the jury known its business, it would have sentenced him to death."

Dawlish tried not to let her impress him too much; he did not want to become dazzled in the light of that first astonishing piece of information, for it might lessen his sensitivity to whatever was to follow.

But Felicity got up, restlessly, and went to the window.

"Alderney let it be known that he is forty-three," said Lady Fripp. "He is, in fact, over fifty. It is twenty-five years ago since he was sentenced to three years' hard labour for this crime. Do you remember the case, Major Dawlish? I—but of course, you don't, you were hardly out of your cradle! His name, then, was Keen."

Dawlish drew a sharp breath; the old woman stared, as if she wondered why that had shocked him.

"His wife was a chorus girl, and he thought she was carrying on with other men. There was one child, a baby girl, ten months old. I remember the case clearly, because my husband was the prosecuting counsel. Alderney, or Keen, returned to his flat one night and found another man there with his wife. He assaulted the man without asking for an explanation, and, according to his story, his wife intervened. She received a blow from which she died. Presumably the jury took into account what is considered to be extreme provocation, nevertheless, such a verdict was a travesty of justice! Don't you agree?" she added, sharply.

"I can see your point," murmured Dawlish.

"You mean you disagree." Lady Fripp sniffed. "One day, Major Dawlish, you and others like you will think more of the victim of such violence than of the perpetrators. After the trial, the wife's complete innocence of intrigue and infidelity was established. Had the jury known of it earlier, the verdict might have been very different. Well, he was sent to prison and the baby was left in the charge of an aunt, who took the child away. I do not think that Alderney ever found her. Until recently, I knew nothing of what happened to Keen, except that he reappeared a little while before the war as Brian Alderney, and had with him a new wife. He must have contrived to forge a birth-certificate, and probably assumed another man's identity, or he would not have been knighted. Well, Major Dawlish, are you satisfied with the information I have given you?"

"Fully," said Dawlish, after a long pause, and then added gently: "But you can give me more, can't you?"

"Such as?"

"Why did you accept the man socially?" asked Dawlish.

Lady Fripp drew a sharp breath.

"Do you think I would have accepted him had I known the truth from the beginning? There was something in his appearance that puzzled me, but it was not until the day after the hold-ups in these country roads that I placed him, recalling all the history of the case. It occurred to me that it would be better to say nothing for the time being. You understand, Major Dawlish, that in the short time that he has been here, he has become *extremely* popular. He has many friends—he has inspired something akin to hero-worship in a great many people who should know better. Oh, be in no doubt about *that*. His position in the county is very strong indeed, and I—" she shrugged her shoulders—"I have the reputation of being an old crank, who is more nuisance than she is worth. I could offer no *proof* at the time."

"Can you now?" asked Dawlish, quickly.

"Yes."

"When did you get it?"

"I employed a detective agency, which traced Keen's movements to Canada, then Australia, later the Dutch East Indies and eventually back to England."

"Did you also have the daughter traced?" asked Dawlish.

"Yes. She lives in Hendon, under her own name, in a small boarding-house, and I understand that she is doing quite well for herself."

"Is she married?" asked Dawlish, heavily.

"No. You seem most interested in this daughter, Major Dawlish."

"I've known for some time that Alderney was searching for a woman," said Dawlish. "Apparently it was his daughter."

"I hope he never finds her," said Lady Fripp, sharply.

"I don't think he ever will," said Dawlish, slowly. So much seemed clear, now. Alderney had searched for his daughter until, on that day, he had thought he had found her. He had gone into the grounds, perhaps, to steady himself for an interview which might be extremely difficult—and then the fire had started. It was little wonder that he had been so distressed, little wonder that his wife had been so upset.

"What are you thinking about?" asked Lady Fripp.

"This story," said Dawlish, and smiled. "Lady Fripp—"

"Yes?"

"Have you any reason at all for thinking that Alderney has committed any crime *since* he returned to England?"

She sniffed.

"Some people would consider that it was a crime for him to return," she said.

"Be just, if you can't be merciful," said Dawlish.

"I have no reason to belive that he has done anything that he shouldn't," said Lady Fripp, "but it is a remarkably convenient time for him to lose his memory."

"What makes you say that?" asked Dawlish.

She sniffed again.

"I told him what I know," she said haughtily.

"You—" began Dawlish.

"I told him that I did not desire him to live at *Akers*, but that I had some regard for his wife's feelings, and would not create a public scandal by going to the police if he would leave."

Dawlish said slowly. "Lady Fripp, will it surprise you to know that Alderney is being blackmailed—has been blackmailed for some time? That he has been forced to employ people with criminal records, and that he has been able to do nothing to defend himself?"

"He has asked for everything that has happened to him," declared Lady Fripp, unforgivingly. "I *know* the whole truth, and that poor child whom he murdered—"

"Is murder so much greater a sin than mercilessness?" Dawlish asked.

"That remark is *not* well-received," said Lady Fripp.

"I'm sorry," said Dawlish, "I only hoped, without really expecting, that it would be. And—I warmly appreciate what you have told me. Why did you choose me, and not the police?"

"I have promised the man that there shall be no scandal if he behaves himself," repeated Lady Fripp, "and I shall keep that promise. I gave him three months in which to leave the district. I hope that you will be able to persuade him to take the sensible course," she added, "and—"

"Suposing he *has* lost his memory?" asked Felicity.

"I do not believe for one moment that he has," said Lady Fripp. "I do not even believe that his wife is lost, in spite of the fuss in the newspapers. I think she has probably discovered the truth, and left him. He would naturally be too vain to accept that simple solution of her disappearance. And now I must go," she added, rising with a queenly air of finality.

Dawlish went with her to the door, and as they reached the porch, they saw a girl walking up the drive.

She was a stranger.

Dawlish did not know why he was quite so surprised, except that few visitors came on foot to *Four Ways*. She walked briskly, and was not far behind Lady Fripp's antiquated Austin.

The chauffeur sprang to the door and opened it.

Only then did Dawlish realise that he had not asked Lady Fripp about her new chauffeur. There would be time for that later. He waved to her as she sat in the back of the car, staring with the privileged frankness of old age at the newcomer.

The girl continued to walk towards the house and Dawlish. She was good-looking, although not pretty, and there was something familiar about her features. "I am told that Sir Brian Alderney is here," she said.

"He is," said Dawlish. He felt a sharp stab of bewilderment as he watched the girl.

"I wonder if I can see him?" asked the girl. "My name is Mary Keen."

Chapter 13

OUT OF THE PAST

Dawlish looked at her gravely, without conveying either interest or curiosity. "He's not too well," he said, leading the way back into the house. "I'm not sure that he will be able to see you."

"I do hope that he can," she said, worriedly. "I have been trying to get to see him for some time, but this has been my first opportunity. I have to go back today."

"I see," said Dawlish.

He moved on into the drawing-room, not knowing quite how to tackle this situation.

"I was told that he was ill when I telephoned *Akers*," said Mary. "It isn't serious, I hope."

"It's concussion after a blow on the head," said Dawlish.

"Oh, an accident," she said, as if relieved.

"It's affected his memory."

"Oh," said Mary.

Felicity took her coat. She wore a well-cut suit, and her plentiful dark hair had recently been set. Obviously she had gone to some trouble over her appearance.

"Are you a close friend of his?" she asked.

"We're quite good friends," smiled Dawlish.

"You must be, if he's staying here instead of his own home," said the girl. "I do hope this isn't a wasted journey—perhaps you can tell me. I have come for an appointment about a secretarial post which he has offered me. Will he remember anything about that, do you think?"

"I'm afraid not," said Dawlish.

She bit her lips in vexation; they were full, well-shaped lips.

"That's wasted my day," she said, and raised her hands rather helplessly. "I have been trying to get a day off to come here for nearly three weeks, and this was the first opportunity. I wrote and told him that I was coming, but I suppose he didn't get the letter."

"He hadn't been reading his post," Dawlish said.

She forced a smile. "Isn't there any chance that he'll be able to interview me?"

"I'll speak to him," promised Dawlish.

"Thank you so much."

"Perhaps if you gave me some details," Dawlish said, "it might help to jog his memory."

"There's not very much to go on," said Mary Keen, slowly. "The whole thing was a little unusual. I had a letter about three weeks ago, asking me if I were interested in changing my employment, and telling me that Sir Brian Alderney was looking for a secretary who would be prepared to live in the country. I have always rather wanted to get out of London, but I have a fairly good job, and I couldn't risk losing it unless I was settled for something else. I wrote and said that I was interested, but couldn't say for certain when I could come to see him. He asked me to write and give him as much notice as I could, and that Saturdays or Sundays were quite convenient. I thought it a little odd."

"I know he wanted reliable help," said Dawlish.

"But why did he select me?" she asked.

Dawlish smiled. "He has his methods! Why didn't you come at a week-end?"

"My employer has been away," said Mary Keen, "and I was on duty practically all the time. This is the first full day I've been able to take off since I heard from Sir Brian. I telephoned *Akers* from the station, and was told he was here. I should have got here earlier," she added, "but I missed the bus in Haslemere and I couldn't get a taxi, so I walked."

"From Haslemere? You need a drink," said Dawlish.

"I'll see to it," Felicity murmured. "You go and see Brian."

Dawlish walked slowly upstairs, deep in thought. Too much had come at once for him to get his thoughts in order, but in one way the happenings were complementary. The mystery of Alderney was solved; the fact that known criminals could force themselves upon him was no longer surprising. He had told Dawlish that he was being blackmailed; the men doubtless threatened a disclosure of his past if he refused to let them stay at *Akers*. With a 'new' life, a 'new' wife and the world before him, it was not surprising that Alderney had thought himself capable of fighting against these influences. The last thing in the world he would want was the disclosure of his first marriage, his trial and sentence.

What trick of fate had sent him here, on the doorstep of one of the few people who would remember him?

Dawlish reached the landing, but did not go to Alderney's room immediately. He went into his own, and sat on the edge of the bed, lighting a cigarette. He could hear Alderney talking to the day-nurse. Would the news that his daughter was downstairs force him out of his silence?

Dawlish did not doubt for one moment that it was his daughter.

So much was obvious, now.

Painstakingly, through a private detective agency no doubt, Alderney had set out to find the girl. He knew that she was known by her real name. He had probably interviewed several 'Mary Keens'. Anyone of that name whose antecedents were the slightest degree doubtful he had seen, either in London or in Haslemere. His long quest for a secretary was now fully explained, and the police would not have thought it odd but for their other suspicions. The girl who had come to see him on the evening of the fire had not been the right girl. He rejected, now, the theory that the Alderneys had gone for a stroll, so that Alderney himself should prepare himself for a trying interview. The story, as he knew it from Alderney, was that he and his wife had been in the grounds when they had been informed of the visitor. They had hurried back at once, only to find the fire.

Why had that fire been started?

Dawlish smiled crookedly. There was no point in asking himself futile questions. The fire was a separate business from the one under immediate review. One fact made him rueful. Twice the police had taken Alderney's fingerprints, so they must know his real name. Probably Trivett and Leven had deliberately held the information back; since he had not obtained results, the Powers That Be probably regretted the impulse to give him information.

He had now to face Alderney. Dawlish worked out what seemed the most likely way of approach, and then got up. On the landing, he heard Felicity talking to Mary Keen.

"Of course you'll stay to lunch," she said. The girl's voice was in a lower key, and he did not hear her rejoinder. Dawlish smiled as he tapped on Alderney's door. The day-nurse, a middle-aged woman, opened the door.

He found Alderney dressed, and sitting in an easy chair. There was a book open on his knees, and he was smoking a pipe. He did not look round, and Dawlish saw his face in the mirror. He had the blank expression which Dawlish had so often seen before, and which, if it were assumed, was a remarkable tribute to his acting powers. He was not trying to read, and he showed no interest at all in his visitor. The nurses reported that he often looked up with the same helpless, lost expression as he was doing now. He had not once called Dawlish by his name; that was one of the reasons why Dawlish clung to the belief that he was acting; whatever he might have forgotten, he should by now have learned to remember the names of the people about him, names which he was hearing a dozen times a day.

Dawlish stood looking at his reflection.

Alderney stirred.

For the first time, Dawlish began to wonder whether he could be mistaken, whether the weight of evidence that Alderney had genuinely lost his memory should be accepted. He was against accepting it; but was that sheer stubborness?

Another thought entered his head: it had come, unbidden, many times. Had Alderney received so great a shock when his wife had telephoned him that it *had* affected his mind?

Dawlish moved forward, and pulled up another chair.

"Hallo," smiled Dawlish. "How are you this morning?"

"I think I am improving," said Alderney, with a slow, reluctant smile. "I am still—troubled."

"I know," said Dawlish. He lit a cigarette, and then added quietly: "Lady Fripp has just been to see me."

"Who?"

"Lady Fripp."

"Indeed," said Alderney.

"She thinks she knows who you are," said Dawlish.

"A great many people seem to be able to assure me that I am

Sir Brian Alderney, who lives at *Akers*, and I suppose the day will come when I will be able to accept that without question. Just now—"

"This is rather different," said Dawlish. "She tells me that she remembers you much earlier than the time when you came to live at *Akers*."

"And where did I live then?" asked Alderney.

"In a London flat," said Dawlish. He tapped the ash of his cigarette. "Doesn't it call anything to mind?"

"Nothing."

"I wish we could help," said Dawlish. He leaned back with his eyes narrowed. "Mary Keen is downstairs," he said, in the same level voice.

He won!

Alderney sat up sharply, and the pipe dropped from his lips. He did not try to retrieve it, although the hot ash spilt over his hand. He raised his hand, but it was not to shake the ash away. The pipe fell on the floor, and he continued to stare glassily at Dawlish. Just as Lady Fripp had succeeded in discomfiting Dawlish, so had Dawlish succeeded in getting past the protective barrier which Alderney had erected about himself.

There would be little point in further pretence now.

"She wants to see you," Dawlish added.

Slowly, as if the movement caused him great pain, Alderney bent down and picked up his pipe.

"Well?" asked Dawlish.

"I don't know what you mean," said Alderney, with a catch in his breath.

"I think you do," said Dawlish. He smiled gently. "I can send her away, Alderney. I can tell her that you're not well enough to see her. I think, with a little trouble, I could make sure that you couldn't find her again. But she's downstairs, waiting, and once she sees you, she'll know that you're not really interested in finding a secretary. The likeness is remarkable."

Alderney drew in a sharp breath.

"Dawlish—" his voice was hoarse.

Dawlish did not speak.

"You're not—lying to me?"

"No, she's here all right."

Alderney closed his eyes.

They sat in silence for a long time, and Dawlish knew that the long struggle with the man was over. Alderney would not pretend again, he would know that the evidence against him was too strong. He would have to face the truth now, would have to submit himself to examination and interrogation. And it seemed that the desire to find his daughter was strong enough for him to overthrow the defensive barrier.

"I would like to see her," said Alderney, slowly, "without her seeing me. Can you arrange that?"

"I think so."

"Will you?"

Dawlish said: "All right, Alderney. But afterwards—"

"Let us get that over first," said Alderney.

It was not difficult to arrange.

Felicity agreed to take the girl into the garden, and pause with her at the flowerbeds beneath Alderney's window.

Dawlish, leaving Felicity, went upstairs again to Alderney's room. The man was standing by the window looking out. Drawn and haggard, he no longer looked a young middle-aged man, but easily the fifty-odd years with which Lady Fripp credited him. He turned to glance at Dawlish.

"Stand by the side of the window," Dawlish said.

He arranged a curtain so that Alderney could look out without being seen if either of the women turned a casual glance upwards, then stood opposite him, watching him closely. There was the sound of footsteps on the gravel path, and then voices. Felicity was saying that she looked after the flower garden most of the time, and Dawlish took charge of the orchard. The girl commented lightly on the blooms beneath Alderney's window.

"They're lovely," she said, with enthusiasm.

Alderney was gripping the curtain, the knuckles of his hand showing white. Dawlish, watching him, could be in no doubt as to the man's feelings.

As Mary and Felicity strolled from sight, Dawlish relaxed. Alderney turned from the window.

"Well?" asked Dawlish, quietly.

"You know who she is, don't you?"

"I think so."

"I thought—"

"You thought she had burned to death," said Dawlish.

Alderney winced.

"Yes. I thought the girl who came to see me that evening *was* my daughter. Everything pointed to it."

Dawlish remained silent.

"Well," Alderney continued, "I've found her. I didn't think it would be in circumstances like these." He laughed abruptly. "I had the foolish idea that, if I found her, I could employ her as a secretary, and more or less adopt her. My wife was quite prepared to help in every way."

Dawlish did not speak.

"This is an admission, of course," said Alderney, "an admission that Lady Fripp told you the truth."

"There wasn't much doubt about that," said Dawlish, "but she didn't tell me everything."

Alderney said slowly: "No, she couldn't do that. But you know quite a lot now, don't you? You know that I've been blackmailed and forced to—obey certain orders."

"Yes."

"You know who some of my servants are?"

"Yes."

"Do you know why the fire was started?"

"No," said Dawlish.

"I'll tell you," said Alderney, and he shivered as he sat down.

The gong boomed through the house, but Dawlish ignored it.

Chapter 14

MUCH IS EXPLAINED

Dawlish did not know how Felicity explained his continued absence to Mary; nor did he worry a great deal about it. It was enough that Alderney was prepared to speak. Dawlish listened without comment or movement until the last word.

"Are you going to see her?" Dawlish asked.

"Yes. A little later," said Alderney.

"Are you going to offer her the job?"

"How can I, now?"

Dawlish said: "Alderney, have you ever thought of telling her the truth?"

"No, I haven't."

"Why don't you?"

"Do you think I want her to hate me all her life?" snapped Alderney. "I'd rather never see her again."

"She doesn't look to me like a good hater," said Dawlish, quietly. "Alderney, supposing everything worked out as you wanted it to, supposing you employed her, and she was living under your roof all the time—do you think you could keep the truth from her indefinitely? Even if no one told her—and people can be very malicious in handing on some piece of secretly discovered information—do you think it would work? Wouldn't she realise that there was something odd? And wouldn't you and your wife find the false position intolerable after a while?"

"I've always convinced myself that we wouldn't," said Alderney.

"Think again," said Dawlish.

There was a long pause, and then Alderney demanded in a harsh voice:

"What are you driving at?"

Dawlish said: "I could tell her the truth, at once. For the time being, if it seemed necessary, we could keep up the pretence that you're ill. It would help, I think. And it would be easier to judge what she really felt about the relationship. The truth is that unless she is prepared to accept you, without flinching from the past, you might as well let her go, and try to forget that you ever wanted her to live with you."

Alderney licked his lips.

"Dawlish—"

"Yes."

"I've dreamed of finding her for nearly twenty-five years. I've paid for her education, I settled money on her through her mother's sister. I didn't know that the sister would keep her from me. Since her aunt's death ten years ago, I've sought for the child. Now—"

"I'm not going to try to force the issue," Dawlish said, "but I think that what I have suggested is the wise thing to do. Look here—we can talk in the dining-room. You can be in the loggia outside the French windows. You'll hear her reaction. You've got to jump the hurdle sooner or later—this is as good a time as any."

"Why are you so insistent?" asked Alderney.

Dawlish said: "The fear with which you have been living, of what casual people, whom you scarcely know or care about, will think of you if your past comes out, will be as nothing to the tension you will undergo, if this girl becomes a member of your household unknowing, unaware."

"I am prepared for it," said Alderney, heavily.

"You may be prepared for your part of it," Dawlish said, "but are you prepared for hers? The shock that any spiteful person might trigger off?" He stood up. "Well?"

"Tell her," said Alderney, in a tense voice.

"I'll send word when you're to come downstairs," said Dawlish. "Chloe will bring your lunch up."

"*Lunch*! How can I *eat*!"

"It's done," said Dawlish airily, "and all the sorrow in the world has never stopped it."

Felicity and Mary were drinking coffee when he came into the dining-room. He apologised for his lateness, finishing his lunch, and then, as Felicity was pouring out his own coffee, ran silently upstairs to give Alderney the signal for installing himself in the loggia.

Back in the dining-room again he picked up his coffee cup and sank comfortably on the arm of a chair. As he drank, he looked steadily at the girl. The more he saw of her, the more he liked her. She had a calmness, a serenity, which suggested a peace of mind which would not be easily disturbed.

"Well, Mary," he said, and she was startled by his use of her Christian name. "He's going to see you."

She smiled, delightedly.

"But it's not quite what you expected," Dawlish went on. "How much do you know about your parents?"

"I do not understand you."

"Just—how much do you know?"

"Very little," she said, in a low-pitched voice. "I've never known them. My mother—died—when I was young." She stood up abruptly, and her voice hardened. "What has that to do with you?"

"Be patient with me," pleaded Dawlish. "You know, don't you, that your father—"

"I know that he killed her," said Mary, abruptly.

"Who told you?"

"My aunt—who brought me up."

"What else did she tell you about him," asked Dawlish quietly, "did she tell you, for instance, that he found the money for your education?"

"She—no." Mary caught her breath. "She let me think that he took no interest in me whatsoever."

"That wasn't true," said Dawlish. "He's been looking for you for a long time. He's built up a completely new life, and he thought that by finding you, by offering you a post in which he could look after you—"

Mary said slowly: "Aren't you being rather cheaply romantic? Almost—novelettish?" she went on, with much feeling in her voice. "He let me go."

Dawlish said: "Wasn't it the better thing to do? With that history, could he expect to bring you up himself? Wasn't he wise to see that you had a fair chance, and then get out of your life?"

She said nothing.

"How bitter do you feel?" asked Dawlish.

Though he could imagine with sympathy Alderney's tensity of feeling, waiting alone for what might come, Dawlish liked the girl still more for her attitude—there was nothing forced or emotional about her, no shuddering pose or weeping sentimentality.

"I haven't thought of it for a long time," said Mary, slowly. "I can't honestly say that I've felt bitter. I haven't felt anything at all. I didn't know either of them. I—I understood that it had been a tragedy in more ways than one, one of those terrible clashes of wills, of circumstances, of personalities the Greeks understood so well, and on which it would be quite beyond the scope of an outsider to pass judgment or opinion." She was well aware of why Dawlish had started to talk like this, she would not need telling that Alderney was her father. "I've wondered what he was really like, my father, and a stranger."

Dawlish said quietly: "Do you want to see him?"

After a long pause, the girl said quietly:

"Yes."

Dawlish walked to the windows, and opened them.

Felicity got up and went to her husband's side. Dawlish did not see Alderney, who was still in a corner of the loggia, but he saw the man's shadow, and he saw the forced calm on Mary Keen's face. He closed the window firmly, then took Felicity's arm.

"Sorry I had to spring it on you," he said.

"What else could you do?"

"Let's go in the other room," said Dawlish. "I've got his story now, and you may as well know that!" He took her into the drawing-room, and they sat down by the open window.

Dawlish was thinking of the couple outside. He knew that Felicity was dwelling on that strange reunion too.

"Well?" she asked at last.

"Lady Fripp's story was true enough," said Dawlish. "When Alderney came to settle here, after he had remarried, he had no idea who she was. It was just one of those bits of very bad luck."

"You could call her that," said Felicity repressively.

"Soon after he got here, he was seen by someone who had

been in prison with him." Dawlish smiled faintly. "Remember Percy's tales of prison life? And Percy's statement that someone in the vicinity is a receiver in a big way?"

Felicity nodded.

"Alderney doesn't know who it was who recognised him, but it was one of the people whom he met in the ordinary course of events," Dawlish said. "It wasn't Lady Fripp, because she admitted that she's only just realised who he was, while the first discovery came within six months of his coming here. After that—" he paused.

"Go on," said Felicity.

"It seems he was visited by several people, all old lags, who, under threat of the truth being told, he was forced to employ. From then on, he received frequent visitors under the guise of applicants for employment. In truth, they came to bring him stolen jewels."

Felicity drew in a sharp breath.

Dawlish smiled faintly.

"No, he wasn't asked to buy them, only to store them. He would sometimes keep them for a year or more, at other times he would be expected to hold them for only a few weeks. While the stuff was still hot, and the police were searching for it, he would have it in his vaults. When it was safe, or when the thieves had a market, it would be taken away.

"Soon after it started," went on Dawlish, "he began to plan to outwit them, to get evidence against these men which he, in turn, could use against them, to blackmail them into keeping away from him. His initial mistake, of course, which he could hardly have avoided, was to start with them at all. The longer he acted as a go-between, the more dangerous and involved became his position. But he was patient, waiting for an opportunity to gain a stronger hold over them than they had over him.

"Then he discovered that one of the thefts had been from a country house where, later, a watchman died. That made a case of murder against them. Immediately, he told them that he would take a chance, and produce this evidence if they didn't leave him alone. He chose the night of the robbery after the ball. They had a great haul, and wanted to leave it in his vaults. He refused, and countered their threats with threats of his own. They took the stuff away. But again he had made a mistake. He let them find out that he kept the evidence in the vaults *and* a copy in his study, and, on the day that I met Percy—"

"They started the fire," said Felicity, slowly.

"Yes. They sent men in from the outside—men who attacked the policeman at Short Hill. That was in order to deceive the police into thinking that it was an outside job. Actually, his staff started the fire. It was completely successful. Everything that he had collected against them was destroyed."

Felicity said: "And he was no better off."

"Not a scrap," agreed Dawlish. "But he still fought on. He realised that if he gave in this time, he would never be able to shake them off. At the time, he believed the Mary Keen who had died in the fire to be his daughter. I think that was really the deciding factor. The fight was on. Their immediate counterattack was to get his wife away from the house on the pretext of coming to see me. Before that, he had tried to get me to help in the hunt, planning to tell me the whole truth, and rely on my help."

"It's a thousand pities he didn't," said Felicity. "How did he know about you?"

"There's a touch of irony about that," said Dawlish. "These crooks he employed told him. They seem to have thought that by telling him of the danger on his doorstep, he would be more careful. They were there, of course, to watch everything he did, all his comings and goings, to make sure that he didn't disclose anything on the telephone. They were nicely placed for that. But they went too far. They told him that I didn't always tell the police everything, and that gave him his opening. I wish I'd agreed straight out, now," he added, slowly.

"With the only information you had at the time, that wasn't possible," Felicity said.

Dawlish shrugged his shoulders. "Well, that's the position as far as I know it now. Alderney shows up fairly well, I think. He's played the fool, but in the circumstances, I don't see what else he could have done."

"Nor do I," agreed Felicity, after a pause.

"Well, it leaves a pretty problem," Dawlish said. "Who is the man who first recognised Alderney? Whose house was made the repository of the jewels stolen at the ball?" He rubbed the bridge of his nose. "And if it comes to that, why does Roland Mortimer work for Lady Fripp?"

"*She* can't be behind it," Felicity said, positively.

"Oh, no," agreed Dawlish, "it's quite impossible—I should think!" He laughed. "No, I'm not thinking seriously of Percy's formidable aunt, but I'm quite sure that there's some connection."

"Aren't you tilting at shadows?"

"Now, come! The victimised nephew and the villain of the piece working under an assumed name for his aunt! As for Percy, I've a feeling that he knew that Roland Mortimer was somewhere in the district, and Percy, if I judge him aright, still has a sense of family loyalty, although he's been disowned. The chief interest for this afternoon, however, is a matter of father and daughter. What do you think she'll do?"

"Nothing foolish," said Felicity. "She isn't the type."

"No," agreed Dawlish. "There's another nasty problem, too—where is Janice Alderney?"

"What did she say to him over the telephone?"

"Didn't I tell you that?" asked Dawlish. "She had been kidnapped. She was being well-treated. The people who held her said that it was not his daughter who had been killed in the fire, but that they knew where his real daughter was, and would tell her everything if he continued to fight. Completely distracted, he didn't know whether to believe them or not."

"I suppose it was then he lost his memory?"

"He said he had to have time to think," said Dawlish. "Too much was happening in too short a time. He had decisions to make, and it would be fatal to choose the wrong ones."

"Does he really think his wife's all right?"

"He says that they know that he'll do nothing at all for them if anything should happen to her. I think that's reasonable enough, don't you?"

"I suppose so," said Felicity.

"And now we can concentrate on the Fripps and the mysterious chauffeur," said Dawlish, with some satisfaction. "Let's go and see what's happening outside."

As they went into the dining-room, the telephone bell rang.

It was Ted Beresford; triumphantly he told them he'd scored a bull. He knew where Roland Mortimer was hiding . . .

Chapter 15

MY LADY'S CHAUFFEUR

"Nice work, Ted," said Dawlish, "and you're only a few hours late."

"Late!"

"I've seen the mystery man," said Dawlish, and gave Beresford a brief outline of what had happened. As he was ringing off, Alderney and Mary Keen walked past the door. The man's face was grave, the girl looked thoughtful.

Felicity joined her husband.

Dawlish grinned. "I'm getting all sentimental," he said, "and this is no time for sentiment! I want to know a lot more about my lady's chauffeur."

"And Percy," said Felicity.

"And Superintendent William Trivett, not to mention Chief Inspector Leven," said Dawlish, a trifle heavily. "I think I'll have a word with William."

"Why?"

Dawlish put in the call, and stood with his hands in his pockets watching the couple walking across the lawn deep in conversation. "Well, for one thing, they must surely know who

Lady Fripp's chauffeur is. Bill's always hedged on the subject of Roland Mortimer, but this is going too far."

"He might not have known."

"The Yard does keep an eye open," said Dawlish, and then added with a grin: "Sometimes!"

The telephone-bell rang.

Yes, Superintendent Trivett was in his office . . .

"Hallo, Pat!" greeted Trivett, with some enthusiasm. "I've been wondering when I was going to hear from you."

"I've been saving it up," said Dawlish.

"Saving what up?"

"My broadside, what else?"

"As bad as that, is it?" There was an echo of laughter in Trivett's voice. "What's worrying you?"

"Lady Fripp's chauffeur."

"Oh-oh! You haven't taken long to discover that," Trivett said, "we didn't know ourselves until yesterday."

"Yesterday," murmured Dawlish. "I see. Information kept on ice for twenty-four hours. There is also the little matter of a man named Keen—"

"How the devil did you find out about that?" demanded Trivett, really astonished.

"I'm glad something's shaken you," said Dawlish, dryly. "I suppose you knew about the search for Mary Keen?"

After a long pause, Trivett said:

"You're an uncanny beggar."

"Uncanny be blowed," said Dawlish. "But why did you keep me in the dark? Fresh orders from the great panjandrums?"

"No," said Trivett. "I thought you had enough to contend with in your cracked knee. News of further developments would only have risked you hobbling about too soon."

Dawlish felt a glow of pleasure and relief. He had feared that

Scotland Yard had already regretted its first impulse to invite his aid, and would in consequence be withholding from him all further information. Some of his pleasure seeped through to Trivett, who smiled.

"Let's forget it," said Dawlish, handsomely. "What else have you been keeping under your hat?"

"Nothing definite," Trivett said, evasively. "How are you now?"

"Fit enough."

Trivett chuckled.

"I'll take your word for it. I'm going to Guildford this afternoon, and I think I'll look you up first. Oh, by the way, how did you get the information about Alderney?"

"He told me," said Dawlish, with relish.

"He—told you?"

"Yes."

Trivett said with a sharper note in his voice: "I hope you haven't been getting too rough with him."

"My dear chap! We're the best of friends! Can I speak off the record?"

"Of course."

"His daughter's here with him, now."

"*His daughter*!—Good God! man, don't you know his daughter died in the fire?"

"Oh, no, she didn't."

There was another pause. Then Trivett's voice came, probing, reviving. "Are you really sure?"

"Yes. I've talked to her and seen her, and the likeness is too great for there to be any doubt," Dawlish said.

"I see," said Trivett, and then added more briskly: "All right, Pat. I'll be out about half-past six."

Dawlish smiled faintly as he replaced the receiver.

"What are you going to do now?" asked Felicity.

"I'm going to see Percy's formidable aunt and talk to her about her chauffeur," Dawlish said. "Coming?"

"No," said Felicity. "I think I ought to stay until Alderney and Mary Keen get back. I've decided to ask Mary to stay the night."

"I don't expect she'll stay, but ask her by all means," said Dawlish. He grinned. "Provided you square it with Chloe."

Driving towards the village, he found himself thinking much more of Alderney than of Lady Fripp's chauffeur. It was now evident that there was a chance of father and daughter reaching an understanding, but Alderney must, at heart, be worried about his wife. It was a curious fact that he had not seemed outwardly perturbed about her; true, he had said that he felt sure that she would come to no harm, and his reasoning sounded plausible—once anything did happen to her, the mysterious leader of the thieves would know that he could expect no more co-operation from him.

Plausible it might be; but Dawlish saw a flaw in the reasoning.

Anyone who was desperately anxious to keep away from the police would realise that, now Alderney was being watched by them, the truth about his past was bound to come out. In any case, there was little point in continuing to use *Akers* as a repository for stolen jewels. The proximity of the police made it too dangerous. It seemed to Dawlish, therefore that Alderney was not likely to be of any further use to the unknown man; that being so, his wife might indeed, be in great danger.

Had Alderney failed to see this?

There was another note of uncertainty in Dawlish's mind—concerning Alderney's explanation of his feigned loss of memory. At first glance, it appeared a shrewd move; it obstructed the police and others when they wanted to question him, but it could not alter the situation, nor lessen the chance of the police learning that he was also Brian Keen.

Had Alderney told the truth about his reasons? Or had he kept some facts to himself?

Dawlish reached the crossroads at Hindhead, and drove straight over towards Grayshott, where Lady Fripp lived. A sudden shower forced him to drive slowly, for the windscreen was almost obscured.

Looking carefully from side to side he saw a man sheltering under a hedge. The man turned his head away, abruptly. Dawlish frowned as he drove on. For a moment he had seen the man's profile too clearly to be deceived. It was Percy Fripp.

He wondered uneasily whether Percy had come on an errand of vengeance. He could not rid himself of the thought that Percy had received a severe sentence largely because of the savage attack he had launched against the chauffeur.

In the drive, he slowed down.

There was no sign of Percy.

He wished that Fripp had not come; his lurking presence introduced a note of uncertainty, of disquiet.

He pulled up outside the big Georgian house. It held the charm of many such residences, but the grounds—he shook his head.

An elderly maid took his card, said that she would see whether her ladyship was in. Dawlish stood in a gloomy hall, looking out of the small window, which was half-covered with creeper. He heard subdued voices. The maid had gone into the room on the right of the hall—

Suddenly there was a shout.

It came from outside the house, a single, high-pitched yell. Silence followed. Dawlish pulled the door open. The maid came out of the room, saying:

"Her ladyship—"

She broke off, in astonishment, for Dawlish was already on the drive. He thought he heard another shout, coming from the side of the house. He raced round the corner. In front of him was the garage, with the big doors open. He squeezed past a standing car to a door beyond. Across a small courtyard there was an apparently disused air raid shelter, approached by a flight of descending steps. On these steps lay the body of Mortimer, his head battered.

"Percy!" exclaimed Dawlish to himself, grimly.

Reaching the man, he went down on one knee, trying to ease his position. It was impossible to judge whether the injuries were fatal.

Lady Fripp had followed him closely, and now, with admirable presence of mind, she called to the shrinking maid.

"Eileen! Telephone for Dr. Morgan at once. Tell him there has been an accident."

"Yes, ma'am."

"Hurry!" exclaimed Lady Fripp.

She led the way by a different route, back to the house, Dawlish, with Mortimer in his arms, following.

"Dawlish!" suddenly screamed a man's voice. "Dawlish, look out—"

Chapter 16

ONSLAUGHT

The voice had undoubtedly been Percy's, but Dawlish could think of nothing but the armed man.

Together he and the injured man slithered to the ground. He lay flat as a pistol shot rang out sharply.

Lady Fripp uttered a sharp cry—either of pain or alarm.

There was another shot. Dawlish could see that one of the men was pointing a gun towards the garage. He caught a glimpse of Percy, running desperately towards the drive.

Crack!

He saw Mortimer shudder. He could do nothing, for he was not armed. If the men cared to use him as a target—

There were two more shots; so they were firing at Mortimer now.

Dawlish *saw* one bullet enter the chauffeur's head, and then heard Lady Fripp give a high-pitched sigh. There was a rustle of sound, and she fell close to him.

This was a crazy business, there must be something that he could do, there must—

He heard a police whistle; the sound had never been more welcome.

He got to his knees.

The assailants were withdrawing, and a uniformed policeman was running alongside the garage. Dawlish thought there was another, just behind him. He looked at Lady Fripp. She waved to him, as if urging him not to worry about her.

He would have given anything for a gun, but even without one he must try to stop the men getting away. There were too many sudden attacks, far too much violence.

The policeman drew alongside him, gasped out something which Dawlish did not catch, and then plunged into the shrubbery. Dawlish followed him.

He heard the sudden throb of a car engine, coming from his right.

Through the heavy, dark foliage he could see a car moving towards the main road. He remembered a gate in the field next to Lady Fripp's house. If the car once reached that, the men would get away.

The policeman joined him, and thrust past him in turn.

"Don't—" began Dawlish.

The warning came too late. The armed men in the car saw the policeman and fired on sight. The range was point blank. Dawlish heard the man grunt, as he slid towards the ground.

Dawlish turned and made for the garage. Only Lady Fripp and her maid were in sight, the maid helping the old woman towards the house. Mortimer lay on the wet grass, staring upwards with sightless eyes.

Dawlish reached his own car.

A tradesman's van was passing, and Dawlish shouted; the driver heard him and slowed down. Dawlish swung his car round in the wide carriage-way, and raced towards the gates. He could not see the other car, because of the thick hedge, but he knew it had not reached the road.

The driver of the van had his door open.

"Can I—"

"Telephone for the police!" snapped Dawlish. "Armed men—hurry."

The driver jumped out of his van, and rushed towards the house.

Dawlish swung into the road.

The three passengers in the gunmen's car were all standing up. It was an open tourer, and was only ten yards from the gate. Dawlish turned his wheel. The tyres slithered on the wet grass of the roadside verge. Crouching as low as he could, he swung the car right across the gate, making it impossible for the other car to get out.

He heard another shot.

Reaching out to open the far door, he crept out. He heard two bullets strike the side of his car. He did not know how many flew over his head. Still crouching, he slipped behind some low shrubs. He felt some satisfaction for the first time; those men would not be able to get away in the car; if the police got cracking at once, they might round them up.

"*We can't do it!*" a man shouted.

"*We've got to!*"

A pause, and then: "*We'll have to run for it.*"

"*Where?*"

"*Scatter, you fool!*"

"*I'm going to get—*"

"*Shut up!*"

Dawlish peered back to the car. The gunmen were getting out. Two of them began to run across the rainsoaked meadow, slipping and staggering as they ran. They would be able to make little progress. If only a cordon could be flung round the vicinity quickly, there would be a good chance of catching them.

"*Mr. Dawlish!*"

That was Lady Fripp. Dawlish straightened up, and saw her in the gateway of her house. The tradesman was standing beside her.

"Hallo there," called Dawlish, sharply.

"I thought—" began Lady Fripp, and then stopped abruptly.

"Have you warned the police?" called Dawlish.

"I've done *that*, sir," said the tradesman, a youngish man with adventure-starved eyes. "I wish I'd got a gun!"

"Even without one you might do good work by hopping along and keeping them in sight as long as you can. When the police get here you will be able to help. I'll go in the other direction."

The tradesman said quickly:

"You take the Hindhead road, sir, I'll go the other way. We'll get the beggars."

Dawlish smiled sympathetically at him. A useful fellow.

Thick hedges often hid the fugitives from sight, but there were glimpses to be seen of them. His two had separated. He saw one coming close to the hedge. Almost at once, there was a single shot.

Then he heard an oath, and guessed that the gun was empty. There was no more shooting.

"That's *much* better," he said, aloud.

One prisoner would be better than none, but he might be wiser to go on to Hindhead, where he would surely get some help. A small car was coming towards him with a man and a woman in it. The driver slowed down, and Dawlish called out that there was a man in the field wanted by the police.

"Is there, by George! Stay here, Phil!" The driver swung the car towards the verge, and jumped out almost before it had stopped. "Which way?" he demanded, and Dawlish warmed towards him.

Dawlish said: "Don't let him scare you with his gun, it's empty."

"Oh-*ho*!" said the young man, with some enthusiasm.

"George!" cried the girl. "I'm coming, wait for me!"

"Look here," said Dawlish, "you'd help no end if you'd drive back to Hindhead, and warn the policeman that four armed men are roaming the countryside. Meanwhile, if George will lend me a hand here, I should be more than grateful."

She looked at him doubtfully.

"Better do that, Sis," said 'George'.

By the time the girl had turned the car and driven off, and Dawlish and his helper had forced their way through the hedge, their quarry was a hundred yards away. But he was tiring rapidly. Dawlish thought: "We'll get this one, anyway."

He wondered whether the others would be caught: why they had killed Mortimer; why Percy had warned him; and what Lady Fripp was doing now.

'George' said cheerfully that he would take the prisoner, who gave in without a serious struggle, to the Haslemere Police Station; and he would pick up his sister at Hindhead. He went off in Lady Fripp's Austin, leaving Dawlish with an impression of a cheerful face and a pair of bright and merry eyes. No word had come from any other source, and the doctor had not yet arrived.

Lady Fripp was sitting composedly in the drawing-room. Before her was a tea-tray and on it a decanter.

She took the kettle off a methylated spirit burner, and poured boiling water into the tea-pot. She made an imposing figure, sitting there with her back to the window and her face in shadow. Dawlish admired her for her coolness. Apart from her one lapse, she had taken this with remarkable calm. He could see that her lips were set, but her hand was as steady as a rock as she poured out tea.

She touched the decanter.

"A lacing of whisky?"

"Not for me, thanks," smiled Dawlish. He sat back in a winged armchair and took a cup of tea. "Thanks. Where is your chauffeur?"

"Where he fell," said Lady Fripp. "No more harm can befall him, poor fellow."

"No," said Dawlish soberly, "that's true enough."

"Can you tell me what has been happening?" asked Lady Fripp, with a sharp note in her voice.

Dawlish sipped his tea, wondering both how to begin, and where to end. He wished she had not asked the question, because he was worried in case her nephew had been responsible for some of the trouble. *Had* Fripp first attacked Mortimer? If so, why had he called out that warning?

"Well?" asked Lady Fripp, in a relentless voice.

"I don't know what lies behind it," Dawlish said. "I know only what happened. These men came to murder your chauffeur."

"Are you sure they did not come to murder *you*?"

"Reasonably so," said Dawlish. "They had plenty of opportunity, and didn't take it. No, they wanted Mortimer."

"Mortimer? My man's name is—was," corrected Lady Fripp, sharply—"Ronald."

"That's what he told you," said Dawlish. "His name was, in fact, Roland Mortimer." He wondered if that would strike a chord in the old lady's mind. It did not appear to do so immediately, and he went on: "I'm not going to try to guess why they wanted him dead. He was attacked, went to take shelter—"

"I see." She poured herself out another cup of tea; apparently she had not brought out the whisky for Dawlish's sake alone.

She sipped with relish. When she leaned back, the light shone on her face more fully, and Dawlish saw her pallor. He wondered whether that was the effect of the strain, or whether something he had said had affected her.

He was greatly puzzled by Lady Fripp.

"I shall have the thing removed," she said, abruptly.

"The shelter?"

"Yes. It was built during the war, of course. Since then it has been used to store unwanted articles, but they must go back into the garage." She was talking for the sake of talking, Dawlish thought, and was not really thinking of the air-raid shelter. "Major Dawlish—"

"Yes?"

"Did you say my chauffeur's name was Mortimer, Roland Mortimer?"

"Yes."

Slowly, she said: "Are you aware of the full circumstances which attended my nephew's trial?"

"Yes," said Dawlish, for the third time.

"Is it the same man?"

"I'm afraid so," said Dawlish.

"The fool!" exclaimed Lady Fripp, with unexpected vigour. "The reckless *fool*! Why do you think it necessary to lie to me, Major Dawlish? Have I created the impression that I cannot take the truth?"

"I don't understand you," said Dawlish.

"Nonsense, man! You know perfectly well that my nephew was in the grounds just now. I saw him myself. I thought that he was coming to beg for help from me, but it is clear to me now that Robert came to take revenge on Mortimer—"

"Robert?"

"My nephew."

"Oh, of course," said Dawlish, and added rather absurdly. "We call him Percy."

Lady Fripp looked at him coldly.

"I am sorry that you think this an occasion for flippancy, Major Dawlish. Tell me the truth. Have you not reason to believe that my nephew came and attacked Mortimer? Is it not true that, even in court, he threatened to avenge himself on the man who, he pretended, had deliberately committed perjury in order to send him to prison?"

"I've no more reason to believe that he came to attack Mortimer than you have," said Dawlish.

"Didn't you come here because you knew my nephew was coming?"

Dawlish smiled. "Certainly not. I came to tell you whom you were employing. I happened to see your nephew outside the house. That is all."

Dawlish did not think that Lady Fripp was convinced; and he did not think it greatly mattered. He wondered whether she would tell the police that she had seen her nephew. If so, it was likely that the police would jump to the same conclusion as she had done, but Dawlish could not get out of his mind the fact that it was the cry from Percy that had saved him from the bullets.

Lady Fripp drew in a deep breath.

"Will that doctor *never* come?" she demanded, and then raised her head sharply. "There is a car."

"I'll go to the door," said Dawlish.

"Thank you," said Lady Fripp. "I am sorry that Eileen, my maid, is unwell. It was a great shock to her. She—" she hesitated, and then smiled frostily. "She saw Robert. She has always had some affection for him, and she is more afraid of the consequences of his foolhardiness than anything else."

The front door bell rang.

As he went to the door, Dawlish pondered over what he had been told. He was not surprised to see Leven as well as the doctor.

Leven had no further news, except what the policeman who had been shot in the shrubbery had told him. The man had been wounded in the shoulder, though not seriously. While the doctor was attending to Mortimer, Leven sat in the drawing-room, listening to Lady Fripp's story.

She did not mention Percy.

Nor did Dawlish.

Leven asked Dawlish if he would be worried if the police guard were removed from *Four Ways*. He did not say so, but obviously he had other urgent work for them.

"No, we'll be all right," Dawlish said.

It was an hour later, when he had reached home, that he learned that two of the gunmen had been caught, and the hunt was still on for others. Why had those men been waiting in the grounds of Lady Fripp's house? Why had they attacked Mortimer? Had Percy been responsible for the first attack? If not, why had he visited the house?

He found Felicity helping Chloe in the kitchen. "Percy dropped a log on Mrs. Arbor's foot, and she's had to go home," she explained. "Well, darling, what is all the excitement about?"

"Excitement?"

"I have heard rumours," said Felicity, austerely.

"Those damned little birds again, how they lie," said Dawlish, cheerfully.

She laughed. "These didn't! George and Phyllis Courtland came half an hour ago, and told us something of what you've been up to. They're coming again after dinner—at least, George is."

"George Courtland—" began Dawlish, and then the truth dawned on him. "Oh, the friendly customer on the road. I've never seen him about."

"He's just home from India," said Felicity, "and his sister lives in London. They were on their way from the station when you stopped them."

"Rather a nice couple," Dawlish reflected.

"Never mind what you think of them," said Felicity, "tell me what's been happening. You'd better have a bath while you're telling me," she added, "you look filthy."

He told her the story as he undressed, and voiced his uncertainty about Lady Fripp and Percy. The news that Percy had been involved, startled and worried her; it had long been evident that Felicity had a soft spot for the little man. Dawlish did not express any opinion, although he said that he would like to talk to Percy before Trivett arrived. As it was now half-past five, there wasn't much time.

"I suppose he is back," he added, suddenly alarmed.

"Oh, yes," said Felicity. "He came in rather sheepishly a little While before you did."

"Send the little beggar up, will you?" asked Dawlish.

"You'd better bath first," said Felicity.

"He can kick his heels in the dressing-room," Dawlish said. "By the way, is Mary Keen going back tonight?"

Felicity laughed.

"No. Alderney persuaded her not to!"

Dawlish pondered lazily over the various aspects of the puzzle as he bathed. He heard Percy tap on the door of the dressing-room, and mused over the man's return. Had Percy taken it for granted that he, Dawlish, would not tell the police of his presence at his aunt's house?

Dawlish put on a singlet and trunks, and went into the dressing-room. Percy was standing by the small window. He turned at once, and smiled charmingly.

"Well," said Dawlish. "So you've got your own back at last."

"I was afraid you would come to that conclusion," Percy said, in a low-pitched voice, "but it is not true, Mr. Dawlish. It is certainly true that, after reflection, I decided to go and see Mortimer, but I had nothing to do with the attack on him, nothing at all."

Chapter 17

ACCORDING TO PERCY

If Percy were to be believed, he had fretted over the appearance of Roland Mortimer until at last he had decided to go and have it out with him. He had not gone into the grounds at once, realising that it would be folly to speak to Mortimer while Dawlish was nearby, so he had stayed outside. He had seen the car turn into the field at the side of the house, and, being curious, had then gone into the grounds. The men had surprised Mortimer, who had rushed from the garage to the shelter, seeking safety. Then Dawlish had appeared, and the men had withdrawn to the shrubbery. Still anxious not to disclose his presence, Percy said, he had waited, hoping that Dawlish's arrival had frightened the men off. Then he had seen them approach the house, had drawn closer, cried his warning, and hurried away.

"I assure you, Mr. Dawlish, that is the whole truth," asserted Percy, earnestly. "You must surely understand why I was so anxious not to be seen. With my unfortunate police record and the circumstances attending it—what would the police have assumed? That I had gone on a mission of vengeance, of course."

"Didn't you think I would recognise your voice?" asked Dawlish.

"My dear sir, how could I allow them to shoot at you without giving you a warning? After your kindness to me—and I may say the first real kindness I have experienced for a long time—I could not go without showing that much gratitude."

"I see," said Dawlish.

He began to dress, and Percy watched him anxiously. Dawlish waited for the man to speak, and was not surprised that Percy's first words, uttered nervously, were:

"Will you tell the police, Mr. Dawlish?"

"Others probably saw you," Dawlish said.

"You cannot make yourself answerable for what others say," said Percy. He came forward, his hands outstretched and a pathetic expression in his eyes. "Will you trust me? I set great store by your regard, by your faith in me."

Dawlish hoisted his trousers.

"I haven't all that faith," he announced.

"Please!" exclaimed Percy.

"I'll leave it for the time being," Dawlish said, "but later in the evening I want all the truth from you."

"You know the whole truth, I assure you!"

"I don't," said Dawlish. "Think it over."

Percy went off, unhappily, and Dawlish smiled faintly to himself. He was by no means sure that Percy had kept anything back, but if there were anything else in the little man's mind, he thought, Percy would be driven to tell him before the day was out.

He heard Trivett's car on the drive.

He saw the Scotland Yard man in the morning-room, not wanting to force Alderney to meet him. Like Leven, he gave Dawlish the impression that, in spite of what he had said over the telephone, he was very pleased with life.

He had heard nothing of the afternoon's adventure.

Dawlish told him briefly, omitting only the reference to Percy. Trivett heard him out without a single interruption, and was silent for some time after he had finished. Dawlish poured out drinks, and Trivett sipped a whisky-and-soda.

"Well?" asked Dawlish, at last.

"I think I can explain Mortimer's murder," said Trivett.

"Oh," said Dawlish, raising his eyebrows.

"While you've been laid up, I have been able to get a bit of information."

"Is there no end to police duplicity?" murmured Dawlish.

"You know why I kept it from you," Trivett said. "We won't harp on that. I take it you do want to know what we've found out?"

"Certainly I do."

"It's simple enough now we know," Trivett said. "Our line was the jewel robberies, of course. We plugged away at it, interrogating all known jewel-thieves, and we made some progress. Flash Ben *was* dissatisfied with his rake-off. That is why he was murdered. And he was planted outside your window as a warning."

"We caught the man Rummy," Trivett went on. "He and Flash Ben often worked together. Rummy introduced Ben to this show. The original plan was to break into some of the big houses during the ball. Twenty men, working in pairs, were to do two or three houses a pair. Then, belatedly, it was realised that many of the women would be wearing their jewels. Plans were changed and the hold-up substituted for the burglaries. When Flash Ben realised how much would probably be taken, he wanted a larger cut. That started the trouble."

"Who killed him?" asked Dawlish.

Trivett shrugged. "Who knows? According to Rummy, the

leader of the men who staged the hold-ups is named Paterson. It's an alias, of course, but we've a description of him, and we're watching known jewel-thieves and cracksmen so cautiously that he daren't make a move. He's hoping that we'll get tired first, and relax some of the precautions. We won't," Trivett added, meaningly.

Dawlish thought that he saw part of the reason for Trivett's satisfaction.

"Where does Mortimer come in?" he demanded.

"Lady Fripp's jewels explain that," said Trivett, with a smile. "No, we haven't been idle, Pat. Mortimer was a rogue—he was once a fence, lost his money, and took to burglary. Recently he'd worked for Paterson. Be ready for a shock," he added.

"I'm ready."

"In practically every big house of any importance in the district, there is a new member of the staff planted to find out where the valuables are kept, I gather from Rummy that Paterson is planning one big swoop—all the houses on the same night. Not bad."

"Not at all bad," said Dawlish. "I wish I could believe it."

Trivett gaped.

"And I'm surprised that you do," said Dawlish, severely.

"Now, look here—"

Dawlish laughed. "Sorry, Bill. But there are gaps, aren't there? Mortimer was one of many, his particular interest was Lady Fripp. The Courtlands, the Maidments and the other families are employing old lags—"

"What's wrong with it?" asked Trivett.

"Most of the women *were* wearing their jewels," Dawlish reminded him. "The haul on that night was terrific, Bill. Some of them may have a few baubles left, but this particular district has been swept clean. And no one in his senses would concentrate all his men on a place where the police are on the alert morning, noon and night. You've been bluffed."

Trivett eyed him sceptically.

"Or have you special inside knowledge?" asked Dawlish.

"I've Rummy's statement," said Trivett, "together with a report from Leven." He touched his pocket. "As a matter of fact, Pat, I'm only in this because the trouble started in London, and I'm giving Leven his chance. I think he'll shine. He's covered every house of any size in the district, and he's got the finger-prints of the servants. Never in the history of Surrey, I imagine, have so many old lags worked in the same small area! The men *are* in the district, don't make any mistake about that."

"I see," said Dawlish.

"I'm sorry to throw cold water on your theory," Trivett went on, "but Leven hasn't been bluffed and nor have I. The men are here and the obvious reason is a concerted series of burglaries. Once it's started—"

"Well?" asked Dawlish, when Trivett paused.

Trivett chuckled.

"Leven *is* good. He's arranged with the local gentry to tele-phone the moment they have any suspicion of trouble. It's reasonable to suppose that the burglaries will all take place on the same night. All will have the help of an inside man. And on that night, after the first warning, the roads will be watched everywhere. It will be the night of the ball in reverse—and the thieves won't get away this time," added Trivett, confidently.

Dawlish ran his finger along the length of his nose.

"Now I see why you and Leven have been so smug," he said.

"Call it smug if you like," said Trivett, "but this little part of Surrey is all sewn up, my lad."

"Horrible confidence of a policeman," murmured Dawlish, "before finding himself flat on his back. Er—could I draw your attention to the ease with which the assailants this afternoon got to work?"

"That's hardly fair," Trivett countered. "We're geared for the main attack. And when that comes, they'll walk into the bag."

"I see," said Dawlish. "What do you think was the cause of the Mortimer murder?"

"I don't know. Could be another case of Flash Ben."

"Meaning?"

"He was preparing to squeal."

"Hum." Dawlish poured out more drinks, and sat down on the arm of a chair. "You may be right about that. What reward would he get?"

"Leniency," said Trivett.

"What crime has he committed?"

"Several, for which we could have held him," Trivett said, and for a moment he looked worried. "As it happened, it would have been better had we done just that. He would at least have remained alive. But we decided that it would be wiser to let him have a run for his money and get him in the bag with the rest."

"If, as you suggest, he meant to squeal, how did the gang find out what he meant to do?"

Trivett shrugged.

"He was the chief witness against Fripp, wasn't he?"

"Oh, yes," said Trivett, and again he looked a little uneasy. "We didn't know at the time that he was mixed up in any earlier funny business, but since you told us to look for him, one or two odd things have turned up. It wouldn't surprise me if Fripp told the truth, and Mortimer did perjure himself. You know the circumstances of the Fripp business, don't you?"

"Yes," said Dawlish. "His books were in a hopeless mess and the money wasn't there to meet his obligations. Fripp said he knew nothing about it and that the money must have been drawn out of his account by forged cheques. Handwriting experts all agreed that the cheques were in fact signed by Fripp himself—and these people don't often make a mistake about hand-writing."

"True enough," said Trivett, "and Fripp's story sounded mighty thin. Mortimer had entrusted a couple of thousand to him, and it was he who blew the gaff. We reconstructed it like this: Fripp was so angry at being found out that he banged Mortimer over the head. Now, it is becoming possible that Fripp knew that Mortimer had jockeyed him into this position, and that he himself was victimised."

"Well, well!" exclaimed Dawlish. "A miscarriage of justice, no less!"

"It doesn't happen often," said Trivett, defensively. "If it's established, there'll be a Queen's Pardon, and—"

"That's not much good to a man who spent five years in jail, since when he's been blackballed by his friends," murmured Dawlish. "Still, he'll be grateful, I don't doubt." He laughed. "Is there really much chance of that?"

"There isn't much doubt that Mortimer was a rogue," said Trivett, "and when one studies the case in retrospect, there was a lot of coincidence. Fripp stuck to his story, but apparently hadn't the wit to realise the significance of one piece of evidence he could have used in his defence. Mortimer did some work for him, and was often in his office. He could have stolen some blank cheques. Forgery is a fine art, and can't always be detected. I'm beginning to think that's how it was done."

"It's a curious business. If Mortimer were charged with other crimes and interrogated about his evidence against Fripp, Mortimer might have broken down and made an admission, don't you think?"

"It's possible," Trivett grunted.

"And he's dead," said Dawlish. "Murdered."

"Why labour the obvious?'

"Someone might prefer Fripp's name still to be mud," murmured Dawlish. "It's just possible—"

"That's enough of *that*," said Trivett, and glanced at his watch. "By Jingo, I must be going!"

Dawlish saw him off, then went upstairs to his bedroom in an extremely thoughtful frame of mind. The possibility that Percy Fripp had been framed for the crime for which he had been sentenced raised many questions. The further possibility that Mortimer had been murdered so that Fripp's reputation should not be re-established loomed large in his mind. He was a long way from satisfied with Trivett's theories, although he had to admit the force of them. He could imagine, too, the zest with which the police were preparing a complete round-up of the thieves after their clean sweep of the district.

Dawlish found one serious obstacle: *would* clever crooks return to the scene of their crime so soon?

The evidence pointed towards it, but to Dawlish it seemed that there might be another explanation of the remarkable activity of habitual criminals in the various households.

Alderney had refused to give temporary storage to the jewels which had been stolen after the ball—and Dawlish could not forget that a substantial haul had been made that night, and the jewels had not been recovered.

Were they still in the district?

Was someone trying to find them?

Were the resident thieves checking up on their respective employers?

If they were, it meant that the organiser of the hold-ups did not know who had the jewels, and was looking for them. They had been taken somewhere for safety, but the main thief did not know where—a curious state of affairs.

Dawlish began to smile.

Felicity came hurrying into the room, a little flustered and hot.

"Hallo, my sweet," said Dawlish. "Anything I can do to help?"

"You can get out my black dress," Felicity said. "Percy's arranging the coffee tray for me. He takes it all so seriously, bless him, and has got it off by heart, who takes black, who takes white. Now my suede shoes . . ." she gave various instructions and Dawlish obediently collected all that she wanted, kissed her on the nape of the neck, and went downstairs.

Alderney and Mary were still talking in the garden. Seeing Dawlish, they came to meet him.

"Did the Superintendent have any news?" Alderney asked quietly.

"About what?"

"About my wife," Alderney said.

"I'm afraid not." Dawlish looked at him steadily; the man's calmness about his wife's disappearance seemed to him an astonishing thing, and again he wandered whether he had heard everything that Alderney could tell him.

Dinner turned out to be a quiet and pleasant meal. There was no restraint; the naturalness of father and daughter should have been surprising, yet Dawlish felt that it was in character.

The sound of a car horn broke the quiet.

"Hallo, who's that?" asked Dawlish, looking up. He saw a two-seater car coming up the drive, and grinned suddenly. "It's George."

"George Courtland?" asked Felicity.

"Yes, and alone—he's left his sister behind."

It was the first time he had been able to study young Courtland, and he certainly liked what he saw of him. He proved to be rather older than Dawlish had thought on the Grayshott

Road. He put him down now as a man in the early thirties. He was fair, not bad-looking, and boyishly eager to help Dawlish.

It was ten o'clock before he left, and soon afterwards Alderney went up to his room. Dawlish left Felicity and Mary together and went for a final stroll round the garden.

Felicity was alone when he returned to the house.

"Has she gone to bed?" he asked, lazily.

"Yes. She's tired, and it can't have been an easy day," said Felicity.

"No. A likeable young woman."

Felicity laughed. "You're not the only one who thinks so."

"George Courtland?"

"The very same."

Dawlish smiled. "Yes, he seemed remarkably interested. Well, it's the way of the world." He lit a final cigarette, and added slowly: "The Courtlands aren't ruled out as possible suspects, you know. George's interest might have a double purpose. It would be quite bright, wouldn't it, to pretend to have fallen for Mary so that he becomes more or less *persona grata* here."

"Darling," said Felicity, "George Courtland is as much a criminal as you are. Let's go to bed!"

Upstairs, Dawlish was quiet for some time. He Said goodnight absently, and then lay awake. He began to toss and turn. He thought that Felicity was asleep, but after a while she stretched out a hand and switched on the bedside lamp.

"What's troubling you?"

"A variety of questions," said Dawlish, looking up at the ceiling. "Chiefly, my own amazing credulity."

"If I can take it, why shouldn't you?" murmured Felicity.

But Dawlish was not to be lightly lifted from a mood of heavy self-analysis.

"And my persistent failure to see one obvious thing," he went on. "It's small consolation that Bill Trivett and Leven don't seem to have done any better."

"Go on," urged Felicity.

Dawlish turned to look at her. "I've been prepared to believe that the Alderney business, the Fripp coincidence and the thefts and plans for further trouble are only indirectly connected. I mean, Percy coming here and finding Mortimer, I've admitted, has nothing to do with the main trouble. Alderney's past history and recent activity, again, are only off-shoots of the real mystery. But there's an over-riding factor which makes nonsense of that—a case of not seeing the wood for the trees."

"Go on," said Felicity, with deeper resignation.

"There isn't much more to say," said Dawlish. "Practically everything has turned on the locality—thieves are in the district in big numbers, Alderney chose this locality, Fripp comes back to the scene of his childhood, if we accept what we're told, all by accident of selection. I doubt it. Then there's the identity of Paterson, who is supposed to be one of the local bigwigs." He broke off, and stretched out for a cigarette. Felicity struck a match for him, and leaned across with it. "Thanks," said Dawlish. "If he is a local man, I think when we find him we'll find that everything else is related."

"How does that help now?" asked Felicity.

Dawlish smiled wryly.

"It doesn't, except in our approach to the situation. I'll have to tackle Alderney and Percy again, and try to find out if they've kept anything back about their reasons for coming to this district. If Alderney had been compelled to come here, for instance—" he sat up sharply. "By George, he may have been forced to select this district." He flung back the bedclothes. "I'll go and see him."

"Leave it tonight," pleaded Felicity, "he must be sleeping the sleep of exhaustion. A few hours can't make any difference, and—"

She broke off abruptly, for something struck the window, and fell to the floor.

Chapter 18

UNEXPECTED RETURN

Felicity jumped. "What's that?"

"I don't know," said Dawlish. "Stay where you are."

He got out of bed and approached the window, bending low. He heard a scattering of small taps on the pane, then he trod on a sharp-angled stone.

Dawlish peered out of the window cautiously. Stones might be the forerunners to bullets. He called out loudly:

"Who's there?"

A woman's voice drifted up to him: "Is that Mr. Dawlish?"

Dawlish pushed the window up, and leaned out. He could see a vague figure outlined against the light gravel of the path.

The voice came again: "Is my husband here?"

"You—" began Dawlish, and then gasped: "Lady Alderney!"

"*What?*" cried Felicity.

"Come round to the front," Dawlish called. "I'll let you in."

Felicity reached for her dressing-gown.

"I'll wake Alderney," she said.

"No, not yet," said Dawlish. "A word with his wife first won't do any harm." He put on his dressing-gown and made for the door.

As he hurried downstairs, his first flush of optimism faded. The woman's kidnappers might be lurking in the grounds. She might have been brought here in order to enable them to force entry without any risk of a fight—and as he reached the front door, he wished that he had a gun in his pocket.

Listening, he heard only the single steps of a woman cross the porch.

He had not switched on the hall light. He hesitated for a moment, then hurried into the sitting-room and climbed out of the window. He slipped silently along the grass verge of the flower bed towards the porch, alert for the slightest sign of danger.

Someone moved further along the path: it was not the woman.

Dawlish stopped abruptly.

He heard Janice Alderney call out: "Oh, *please* hurry!"

That sounded as if she thought she was alone, but was afraid that she was being followed; it seemed a reasonable possibility.

Dawlish watched the path. His trained ear could hear the furtive movements of some watcher who wished to remain unseen. He waited in the shadow of the house. He could hear Janice tapping agitatedly on the door. He did not move. Felicity would be wondering What was keeping him; he hoped that she would not show herself.

Whoever was approaching was a small man.

He drew much nearer.

'Well, well!' thought Dawlish. 'It's Percy!'

Dawlish let him get a couple of yards ahead, and then stepped after him. Stretching out, he seized an arm in a lightning grip, placing a hand over his mouth. A stifled gasp broke the quiet, and Janice swung round.

"What's that?"

"It's all right," Dawlish said, reassuringly. He freed Percy's mouth, but still kept a hand on his arm.

Then he realised that he had not got a key, and called out:

"Fel!"

"Coming!" called Felicity.

The hall light was suddenly switched on. It shone on Janice Alderney, and on Percy, who was shivering, less with cold than with fright, thought Dawlish. He heard voices inside the house, followed by footsteps as Felicity hurried down the stairs.

The door opened.

"Not too wide!" exclaimed Dawlish.

There was still a chance that others were lurking in the grounds, and bullets had flown too often of late to take chances.

Janice slipped into the hall. Dawlish took a firmer grip on Percy's arm, and followed. Nothing happened. Dawlish was not really happy, even when the front door was locked again, and all of them stood in the hall.

Mary Keen had come down the stairs; it was she to whom Felicity had been talking.

Now he could see that Lady Alderney was very pale. She had obviously taken the short cut from the village. Her shoes and stockings, made for town wear, were thickly covered with mud. Leaves stuck in her hair, and her hat was awry. There was a little tear in the coat of her green suit.

Dawlish said reassuringly, "I will fetch your husband."

Felicity gently guided her into the kitchen, and soon Dawlish heard the click of the electric kettle being plugged in.

All this time, Percy had remained quiet.

Dawlish looked sternly into his face.

"Well?" he demanded, sharply.

"Isn't it explanation enough that I thought it possible that someone was going to try to force entry, and I felt it encumbent upon me to watch?"

"It could be, and then it couldn't," said Dawlish, sceptically.

"Why is it that the truth is always more difficult to believe than a lie?" asked Percy despairingly.

"Wait here," said Dawlish, brusquely.

He left the man in the hall and hurried upstairs to Alderney's room.

The man was asleep; Dawlish could just hear his regular breathing, which seemed to sigh in harmony with the gentle wind which moved the curtains.

Dawlish went forward slowly.

He was thinking mostly of Percy, whose explanation was plausible enough. The little man might really be grateful for what had been done for him, and take it on himself to be watchful at night. The police had certainly been withdrawn, but there was no certainty that the danger had done likewise.

He switched on the bedside light, but Alderney did not stir. He touched the man's shoulder.

"Wake up, Alderney," he said.

Alderney still did not stir.

"Wake up!"

Alderney's body lay still.

Dawlish looked down, his lips tightening. The face was very pale—almost chalk white. Dawlish leaned forward and lifted his eyelid. The pupils were pin-points.

He felt the man's pulse; it was slow. There was no doubt that this was a drugged sleep. He would have to send for a doctor; he must take no risk. He hurried to the landing, and called down to Percy.

"Telephone for Dr. Morgan, Percy." He added in a lower key: "Tell him, a possible case of drugs."

"At once, Mr. Dawlish!"

Dawlish went back into the room, but it was a pointless visit; there was nothing at all he could do. He did not think there was any serious danger for the man but, if there was not, why had he been drugged?

And who had drugged him?

It was possible that he had not been sleeping well, and after the exertions of that day, had taken a heavy dose of sleeping-pills—but that was all guess work. The immediate problem was to break this news to his wife without alarming her too much.

Dawlish went into his own room and slipped his cigarette-case into his pocket. Then he hurried downstairs.

Percy was moving away from the telephone.

"The doctor has promised to come out at once, sir," he said. "I—I hope that nothing is seriously amiss."

"So do I," said Dawlish. "Fripp, there's something you haven't told me, and I'm not going to let you get away with it."

"But—"

"Why did you really come to this district?" Dawlish demanded.

He did not quite know why he was so desperately anxious to find out the truth now, but before he went in to see Janice Alderney and Mary—who might be just as badly affected as Alderney's wife—he felt that he had to clear up one mystery.

Percy blinked his eyes.

To Dawlish, that seemed a tacit admission that something was being kept back.

He shook him gently.

"Out with it!"

"It is really of no consequence," Percy asserted rather weakly. "I—I thought it possible that Alderney was the man for whom the others were working. I knew that he employed criminals on his staff, I thought it might be that he pretended that he did not know, and actually was fully aware of it."

"What made you think that?"

"I knew his history," said Percy, slowly.

"*You* knew?"

"Yes. I knew he was Brian Keen."

"How did you find out?"

"Eileen, my aunt's maid, told me," said Percy. He sniffed. "I did not see how this could help you, Mr. Dawlish, it was, after all, only guesswork and you are not a man who has much patience with mere conjecture. Eileen knew who Alderney was before—before I was sentenced. I thought that he was living a new life, that it was wrong that he should be made to suffer because of something that had happened twenty-five years ago, and so I held my peace."

"I see," said Dawlish, slowly. "So your aunt's maid knew about Alderney all the time. Did she tell your aunt?"

"She did not!" exclaimed Percy. "She discovered this, as I have said, a little while before the disaster which befell me. We agreed that she should not be told the truth about Alderney. You yourself had discovered the truth about him, hadn't you?"

Dawlish nodded briefly.

"But I did not think it right to tell you," said Percy. He sighed. "So much harm is done by information unrighteously given that I would not be a party to it."

Dawlish looked at him thoughtfully. There was something to be said for his reticence; and, if his motives were what he declared, it was a matter for praise rather than condemnation.

Footsteps sounded in the passage leading to the kitchen. Before either of the men spoke again, Felicity appeared. She looked surprised to see them together, and hesitated.

"Pat—"

Dawlish turned, and gave Felicity a quick, bright smile.

"Hallo!"

"*Do* fetch Alderney," said Felicity. "I don't know what's the matter with his wife, but she's almost distracted—and she won't rest until she's talked to him."

"Then she won't rest for a long time," said Dawlish, heavily.

Chapter 19

JANICE ALDERNEY

Janice Alderney stood by the kitchen table. There was an untouched cup of tea in front of her. Mary Keen stood by her side, tall and grave—more beautiful than her step-mother, yet nothing like so attractive, in spite of Janice's pallor and her feverishly bright eyes.

Janice turned sharply, as Dawlish came into the room.

"Where is he?" she demanded.

Dawlish looked at her with a grave smile.

"He's still asleep," he said.

"Asleep! But I must see him, I tell you!" She turned impulsively towards the door.

"A drugged sleep," Dawlish said quietly. "Did he take morphine, do you know?"

She looked as if she had been struck a physical blow.

"*Drugged?*"

"I don't think it's serious," Dawlish assured her, "and purely as a precaution I've sent for a doctor, but—"

She screamed!

She opened her lips wide, and closed her eyes, and the scream was ear-splitting. She screamed three times. Felicity pushed past

Dawlish and took her shoulders, Mary moved quickly to her other side; and she screamed again.

"Don't—" began Mary.

Quickly, efficiently, Felicity slapped her sharply across her cheek. It was not a powerful blow, but enough to check the rising hysteria. The scream was cut short. Lady Alderney drew a deep, gasping breath.

"Smelling salts indicated," murmured Dawlish.

"Can I get them?" Mary asked, quickly.

"She'll be all right," said Felicity.

She helped Alderney's wife to sit down on a kitchen chair. The woman had not lost consciousness. Her eyes were open, and they held a hopeless look, one of utter desolation. She sat staring at the table, her breathing harsh and uneven, and as he watched, Dawlish wondered whether she was acting.

Though possible, he did not think it was likely. The pitch of nervous tension seemed understandable enough.

She began to shiver, shaking from head to foot uncontrollably.

Dawlish said: "I'll get her a spot of whisky."

As she drank a sip or two, colour slowly returned to her cheeks. She made a tremulous attempt to smile.

"I—I'm sorry."

"That's all right," smiled Dawlish. He pulled up a chair and sat opposite her. "Your husband isn't seriously ill, you know."

"You aren't sure of that," she said, hopelessly.

"I'm very nearly sure."

She closed her eyes. As she sat there, the front door bell rang suddenly, the corresponding bell in the kitchen jangling so violently, that it startled them all.

"The doctor," said Dawlish.

Felicity was out of the room before he had finished speaking, Mary Keen following her.

Alone with Lady Alderney, Dawlish said gently: "What's worrying you?"

She drew a sharp breath.

"They—they said he would die before I saw him," she said. "They said I wouldn't see him alive again. I—Mr. Dawlish! I must see him, I must see him *now!*"

Dawlish took her hands.

"I'll give you one assurance," he said, "he won't die tonight. I don't think he's been heavily drugged. As soon as the doctor comes down. I'll take you up to see him. That's a promise."

She said slowly: "How can you be sure he won't die?"

"Because I've just left him," said Dawlish, "and I've seen enough dying men to know that he's in no immediate danger." When she made no comment, he asked again: "What *is* worrying you? What has happened to you?"

She began to talk, in quick, disconnected sentences.

She believed that Dawlish had sent for her on the Sunday evening when she had left her house, but her car had been held up and she had been taken to a London flat. The man who had talked to her had called himself Paterson. Well fed, well cared for, she had not been threatened, nor had she known for some time why she had been kidnapped. After she had been there for a few days, she had been told to speak to Alderney on the telephone. Dawlish's interest quickened at that stage; would she explain what she had said and corroborate Alderney's statement?

She did.

After that, she had been cared for with the same consideration. Paterson had not asked her for any information, but had made it clear that he was using her to force Alderney into doing what he wanted.

That day, she had been taken from the flat, and driven, in her own car, to Haslemere.

Paterson had come with her.

On the way, he had told her that he had no further use for Alderney, but that it was possible that Alderney knew too much and would be dangerous if he were left alive. Callously, he had told her that he would be dead by the time she reached him. She had been told, also, that he was at Dawlish's house, and she had been put down at the end of Alum Village, and left to get to the house as best she could. She had rung the bell, but not been heard; then she had seen a light at a window, and thrown stones to attract attention.

She had wanted desperately to see her husband, she had been able to think of nothing else; and when Dawlish had told her that he was in a drugged sleep, she had completely lost her self-control.

"I see," said Dawlish, gently. "Well, you needn't worry about your husband, he isn't going to die. Paterson made a mistake—and not his first by any means."

"I don't see how you can be so sure."

"Take my word for it," said Dawlish, and then asked casually, as if it were of little consequence: "What is Paterson like?"

She frowned, trying to concentrate, to bring her mind back to a detail she thought irrelevant.

"Well—there isn't anything remarkable about him."

"Just an ordinary man?"

"That describes him fairly well—medium height, middle-aged, going grey. He looks pleasant enough."

"Can you remember nothing distinctive?"

She shook her head, adding lamely that he was rather faded and nearly always looked tired.

"You'd recognise him again, wouldn't you?" asked Dawlish.

"Yes, yes." Janice brushed the question impatiently aside as Felicity and Dr. Morgan came into the room.

The doctor started at the sight of Janice.

"Why, Lady Alderney!"

She stood up. "How—how is he?"

Morgan covered his surprise. "Er—well, my dear, I don't think there's any need to worry about him," he assured her. "He'll sleep well into the morning, in fact he might not waken until the afternoon, but he'll be all right when he does come round."

"Are you—*sure*?" There was passion in the question.

"I'm as sure as a doctor can be," Morgan assured her, with a professional laugh. "I—" he hesitated, and then took her hand. "I'm much more concerned about *you*."

"*I'm* all right."

Morgan said: "We'll see."

He was a portly man, and obviously he had dressed in haste. He looked tired, too, as he held Janice's hand warmly, sympathetically, in his own.

"How have you been sleeping?" he asked.

"Not very well."

"You need to sleep the clock round," Morgan assured her. "I'll see that you get something to send you off in no time. You've nothing to worry about, neither has your husband, you can set your mind at rest about that."

"Thank you," said Janice.

"Is there a room here?" asked Morgan, of Felicity.

Dawlish spoke quickly.

"Let Janice share your room, Fel."

It was the only thing to do, obviously. Soon Janice was upstairs, and Felicity and Mary were helping her to undress. Morgan had some veronal tablets in his case, and gave them to Dawlish as they stood in the hall. He was obviously still shaken by the return of Lady Alderney.

"Did *you* find where she was?" he asked.

"No," said Dawlish. "She was released some time this evening, I gather. And that reminds me—I'll have to tell the police."

Morgan nodded absently. "Er—Dawlish."

"Yes?"

"Do you know whether Alderney drugged himself?"

"No," said Dawlish.

"It's just possible that he had some morphine," Morgan said, worriedly, "but he's had a pretty heavy dose, I imagine. Is there any possibility that someone else drugged him?"

"It's another matter for the police to investigate," Dawlish said.

"I'm glad you realise that they will have to be told," said Morgan. "Do you keep morphine in the house?"

"Good heavens, no!"

"That's one avenue cleared," said Morgan with some relief. "I take it that you are going to telephone the police now?"

"I am," Dawlish said.

He did not telephone Leven's home, but left word at the police-station. He had little doubt that Leven would send a man out to take a statement from Lady Alderney and to inquire into the administering of the morphine, a most puzzling business, to Dawlish's way of thinking. Alderney might, of course, have taken it himself, or—Mary Keen might have given it to him.

That was a distasteful thought.

Percy Fripp, must, too, be listed among the possible suspects.

It was not until after Leven and a sergeant had come out, got their statement second-hand—for Janice was asleep by the time they arrived—and made the routine inquiries about morphine, that another possibility entered Dawlish's head. He had brought down some blankets and a pillow, and made up a bed on the settee, and was dousing his last cigarette, when the thought occurred to him.

George Courtland had been in the house; it was just possible that he had managed to give Alderney the drug.

"No, that's too far-fetched," Dawlish decided.

The clock in the hall struck the half-hour; it was half-past two. He switched off the light and was soon asleep, but his last thought was that the Courtland family, by merely living in the district, must automatically be classed among he suspects. Courtland had acted quickly when Dawlish had asked for help, and then shown a great interest in Mary Keen.

Was his interest really in Alderney's daughter?

Or had he some other reason for wanting to come to the house?

Dawlish remembered, vaguely, that the possibility had occurred to him before. He was still disinclined to take it too seriously, but it had to be considered.

They all slept late next morning.

The first Dawlish knew was the clattering of the lawn-mower. He lay between sleeping and waking, surprised to find himself in the sitting-room, and then remembering what had happened. It had been a full day, and there was promise of another, equally full. Some questions were answered by Lady Alderney's return, but others took their place; why *had* Paterson let her go?

There was another question which Dawlish had not thought of the night before. Paterson had told Janice that she would not see her husband again. Did that mean that he knew in advance that Alderney was to be poisoned?

How was the man this morning?

He got up, and put on his dressing-gown, and as he did so the clock struck ten.

He could hear sounds coming from the kitchen, and the lawn-mower was still clattering.

On the landing, he met Felicity coming from the bathroom, fully dressed.

"Good-morning, my sweet!"

Felicity kissed him. "Ugh," she said, "shave at once, sir."

"Who's next for the bathroom?"

"You, if you're quick. Mary's up."

"And the others?'

"Both asleep," Felicity told him. "Alderney's no worse than he was last night."

Dawlish took her word for it, bathed and shaved, and then stole into his room, without waking Janice Alderney, to get his clothes. She was sleeping heavily, with one bare arm over the bedspread. Sleep had eased the worried lines from her forehead and her mouth; she looked younger—as young, thought Dawlish, as Mary Keen.

Felicity, Mary and Dawlish breakfasted in the morning-room, and had surprisingly little to say. There was nothing as yet in the papers about Lady Alderney's return. Soon after they had finished, however, the telephone bell rang—Colonel Maitland was inquiring whether it were true that Lady Alderney was safely back. His was the first of a dozen calls. Lady Fripp was remarkable because she did not inquire, although probably she had been among the first to hear the rumour. Dawlish, wondering who had spread it, discovered that Percy had told the gardener who had told the postman. There was no further need for explanation.

Why had Percy been so eager to talk? Dawlish wondered.

He was tired of imputing motives to Percy, and he watched the man working in the garden, as if he were enjoying himself. He was weeding industriously. He seemed thoroughly content with this new life, but Dawlish wondered how long it would satisfy him.

He wondered, also, whether there were any reasonable chance of a rapprochement between aunt and nephew. Certainly not, unless it could be proved that Percy had been wrongly convicted.

Proof of just that came more quickly than Dawlish had expected. It came in the person of Trivett, who arrived at noon with Leven. At first, Dawlish thought that Trivett had come to check Lady Alderney's story; and that was, in fact, part of the reason for the Yard man's arrival.

"How is she?" asked Trivett.

"Not too bad."

"And Alderney?"

"It wouldn't surprise me if he comes round before long," Dawlish said. "I've had a look at him, and I think he's sleeping more lightly. Curious business, isn't it?"

"*Very*," said Trivett, heavily. "Do you know who gave him the stuff?"

Dawlish told him everything that had happened, and the various suspicions that had passed through his mind. Dawlish was not altogether surprised when Leven pooh-poohed the suggestion that George Courtland might be concerned in it; Leven repeated that Courtland had been out of the country for several years, and there was no doubt that it had been pure chance that he had met Dawlish on the road the previous after-noon. He had left the station only a quarter of an hour before, having arrived at Southampton that morning.

"You can cut Courtland out," said Leven. "I can't answer for his father, of course, but I'm pretty certain the whole family can be written off."

Trivett laughed. "Bear up, Pat, I've some other news for you."

"What's that?"

"Roland Mortimer did perjure himself, and Fripp did not embezzle his client's money," said Trivett.

Dawlish looked delighted.

"Well done! Can you establish it?"

"Yes, from papers which Mortimer kept at his London flat," Trivett said. "He kept a diary—"

"Foolish fellow!"

"Not so foolish," said Trivett, and chuckled. "He was being forced into crime, Pat—blackmailed, as it were, because of a minor sin in his young days. He thought the day might come when he would have to turn the tables, and he kept this record."

"*That* ought to be useful," Dawlish said.

"Up to a point it is," admitted Trivett. "He's confirmed what we already know. There is to be another wholesale series of burglaries about here—and," added Trivett, "if we read between the lines, we can take it for granted that he was getting difficult and was killed to shut his mouth. Some of the comments in the last entries in his diary suggest that he was threatening disclosure of Peterson's true identity unless he were given a bigger cut in the proceeds."

Dawlish said sharply: "Does he give Paterson's real name?"

"No," said Trivett, slowly. "That's one thing missing."

"In a diary of that nature, it's a curious omission," Dawlish commented.

Trivett shrugged. "Well, there it is! But we need no more telling, Pat, that Paterson's employer lives around here, and that this final coup is coming off."

Trivett and Leven were then taken up to see Janice, and while they were with her, Felicity hurried downstairs in some excitement to say that Alderney was awake.

"*Now* we're getting somewhere," exclaimed Dawlish.

He dashed up to Alderney's room, before the police could be

told, warned him that Janice was back, and watched him closely. Waking up from his drugged sleep, Alderney would not have such complete control over himself as he usually showed, and might make a disclosure of some importance.

All Dawlish could judge was that he was delighted by the news.

"Not that I ever thought she was in real danger," said Alderney. "I didn't think they would act too rashly." He smiled as if with real satisfaction, and then asked: "But what happened to me?"

Dawlish told him; and he watched Alderney's growing consternation with a curious feeling of disquiet.

Chapter 20

DAWLISH CALLS HIS FRIENDS

"So they're trying to kill *me*," said Alderney, slowly.

Dawlish did not speak.

"What drug was used?" asked Alderney.

"Morphine," said Dawlish.

Alderney closed his eyes.

"So that's what beat them," he said, and when Dawlish asked him sharply what he meant, he said slowly: "I've taken morphia fairly regularly as a sleeping draught. I'm used to it. A dose that would have killed a man who'd never touched it only put me to sleep. Do you know who—"

Dawlish shook his head.

"It must be someone in the household," Alderney said.

"Or with access to the house," amended Dawlish. "Did you take any tablets last night?"

"No, nothing at all—I was tired out. As a matter of fact," went on Alderney, "I was so overwhelmingly tired, that I came to bed early. It *must* have been in my food, Dawlish!"

"Or drink," mused Dawlish. "I—" he stared at the man in astonishment, for Alderney had suddenly sat erect, and was staring at him as if in horror. "Now what's the matter?" he demanded.

Alderney did not answer.

"What is it?" demanded Dawlish, sharply.

Alderney said in a hard voice:

"What *is* your interest in this business, Dawlish?"

"Rather more than interested spectator," said Dawlish, "and I—"

He broke off.

There was a tap at the door, which opened before either of them spoke. Trivett and Leven came in, and, judging from Trivett's expression, he was not too pleased that Dawlish had arranged to see Alderney without him. Leven also sent a sharp glance at Dawlish, who was so preoccupied with Alderney's change of manner that he hardly noticed it.

Trivett spoke quickly:

"Are you all right, Alderney?"

"I—am, yes," said Alderney. He was breathing in quick, shallow gasps, and still staring at Dawlish with the look of horror in his eyes. "Superintendent, it *is* known that a criminal of—of exceptional cunning lives in this district, isn't it?"

"Yes."

Alderney said: "*Isn't it time you questioned Dawlish?*"

Dawlish sat very still.

Trivett said: "Mr. Dawlish is—"

"Trusted by the police, by everybody!" cried Alderney. "No one dreams of suspecting him. Hasn't it occurred to you that with such an impeccable reputation he is in a perfect position to do what he likes?"

Alderney was antagonising Trivett, Dawlish thought; but Leven bent a curious, half-suspicious glance at him.

"Hasn't it?" demanded Alderney.

"Now listen to me," began Trivett.

"You listen to me!" cried Alderney. "He refused to help to search for the thieves. He was the only one who managed to save any of the jewels. Wasn't that remarkable? Can you be sure he didn't arrange it beforehand? Everyone trusts him, this is the last house in the world you would think of searching for the stolen jewels—why don't you search it?" He was breathing heavily, as if the accusation were taking a lot out of him. He looked hard at Dawlish, who still sat quite still. "And why don't you search for the morphine? It was in something I ate or drank last night—wasn't it?" he demanded, harshly.

"Yes," said Trivett, slowly.

"Don't stand there gaping at me, start searching!"

"I think—" began Trivett again.

"Oh, he's a friend of yours, he's a friend of authority, that's what strengthens his position. But nearly everything has happened from this house. It was a message from here which lured my wife away. And—"

Leven said: "Paterson knew that there would be an attempt to poison Alderney." He was speaking to Trivett but looking at Dawlish. "That's so, isn't it, Superintendent?"

"Yes," said Trivett.

"And Paterson told Lady Alderney to come here, so he knew that Alderney was staying here—"

"It was Dawlish who insisted on it, he wanted me under his eye, he wouldn't let me go to my own house," Alderney cried, and there was a sob in his voice. "He was at the house on the night of the fire, too—what was he doing there? Oh, he's fooled you, he's fooled us all! He's so careful that when my daughter came yesterday he persuaded her to stay overnight, he didn't want anything to go wrong. *Are you going to search the house?*"

Dawlish saw Trivett's dazed expression. It was not surprising.

In his heart, Trivett knew quite well that there were no grounds for this outburst, but as a policeman he must assess the evidence.

Leven was doing that; and his manner told what he was thinking.

"And—there's Fripp," Alderney went on. "Why is Fripp staying here? He's a rogue, he's just come out of jail—Dawlish knows it. Did *you* know that?" he demanded.

"Fripp?" asked Leven, sharply.

"Do you mean Robert Fripp?" asked Trivett.

"The man Dawlish calls Percy, the tramp who was always hanging around, why is he here, in Dawlish's house? *Did you know?*"

"No," said Leven.

Trivett asked slowly: "Is Robert Fripp here, Pat?"

"Oh, yes," said Dawlish.

"Why didn't you tell us that?"

"He didn't want you to know!" snapped Alderney.

Leven drew a deep breath.

"Hadn't we better see Fripp, Superintendent?"

"You'd better have a look round," Dawlish said. "Alderney won't be satisfied until you've done that *and* found nothing. Help yourself," he added, and stood up, looking at Alderney with a quiet smile. "I wonder how sincere you are about your accusations," he mused. "You wouldn't be trying to pass the buck, would you?"

Alderney said: "*Someone* is behind all this."

Trivett stood up, looking at Dawlish with an expression which seemed to say: "You've played the fool too much, you ass, you should have told us about Fripp." Dawlish was fully prepared to agree. They went towards the door, and Alderney called out:

"Send my wife here, will you?"

"Yes," said Trivett.

On the landing, Trivett looked at Dawlish, and said in a quiet, rather puzzled voice:

"You know we'll have to search, don't you?"

"Of course," said Dawlish. "The sooner the better."

He went downstairs ahead of them, and turned into the drawing-room. He sat down for a few minutes, smoking, looking out on the freshly cut lawn. He was smiling, without amusement. Looking at the situation dispassionately, he had to admit that there appeared to be something in what Alderney said. His great mistake had been to allow Percy to stay here without telling the police. True, there was no evidence that Percy was mixed up in this business, beyond a certain coincidence, but—

Dawlish narrowed his eyes.

He had kept silent about Percy's presence at Lady Fripp's house at the time of Mortimer's murder. That would probably come out, and if it did the circumstances would look bad indeed.

He lit another cigarette.

Leven was walking in front of the house, with a hand on Percy's arm. Percy was protesting volubly, but Dawlish could not hear what he said.

Felicity came in, so quietly that Dawlish started when he heard the door close.

"What's gone wrong?" she asked.

Dawlish jumped up. The sight of Felicity's worried face cheered him up, for some odd reason, and he put an arm about her shoulders and said:

"Nothing serious, my sweet, except that I've become Suspect Number 1."

"I rather thought so, from what Leven was saying to Percy," said Felicity. She did not smile.

"Oh, come! That's nonsense!"

"But will the police think so?"

"My dear girl," protested Dawlish, "Bill Trivett—"

"Will have to do the obvious thing," said Felicity. "I haven't said anything to you, Pat, it would have sounded crazy, but one thing and another *has* rather pointed to us. I mean, keeping Alderney and Percy here, and—I suppose that's what Leven picked on," she added abruptly.

"Alderney did the picking," said Dawlish. "I wonder if the beggar was trying to switch attention on to me."

He grinned.

"It isn't funny," Felicity said. "Pat—"

"You're taking this far too seriously."

"Am I?" asked Felicity. "Pat, you did put a serious spoke in their wheel, didn't you, when you recovered so many of the jewels. They haven't any reason to love you. Now Alderney's clear, they'll want the police to find a scapegoat."

"I suppose so," admitted Dawlish.

"You know it's true. Pat—could anyone have *planted* some of the jewels here?"

Dawlish said in amazement: "*What's* that?"

"Answer me," said Felicity.

"Yes," said Dawlish, slowly, and then repeated more briskly: "Yes, they could. It hadn't occurred to me. I think we'd better take out an insurance, don't you?"

"What do you mean?"

"Send for Ted and Tim," said Dawlish. He laughed, but there was a strained note in his voice. "After all, before we know where we are, I might be in the lock-up!" He kissed her lightly, and went into the hall.

A policeman was standing on duty near the door. He looked at Dawlish without expression.

Dawlish lifted the telephone.

The operator answered, and he gave Ted Beresford's number.

He felt like laughing at the absurdity of the situation, but had an underlying feeling of anxiety. The way in which Alderney had flung that accusation at him was worrying; the man *might* know that something was hidden in the house, the outburst might have been cleverly calculated to force the police to search and find—what?

A car sounded on the drive.

The telephone bell rang as George Courtland came cheerfully in to the hall.

"Hallo, hallo," he said. "'Morning, Dawlish—or is it afternoon?" the man's geniality seemed forced—but then, admitted Dawlish, any geniality would seem forced to him at that moment. "Where's everybody?" asked George, and then apologised: "Sorry—go ahead."

"Thanks," said Dawlish, dryly.

Joan Beresford answered the telephone.

"Hello, Pat. How are you all?"

"Doing fine," said Dawlish, a trifle heavily. "Is Ted in?"

"No, but he should be in to lunch."

"Ask him to drop everything and come down here, will you?" asked Dawlish. "And bring Tim with him. I might have to go away for a day or two, and there'll be a lot to do while I'm gone."

Joan, who knew that Dawlish would not make the request unless it were important, said quietly:

"Of course, what's the trouble?"

"Temporary suspicion of the Dawlish *menage*," said Dawlish, lightly.

"*Pat!*"

"Only temporary," Dawlish assured her. "I must ring off, old girl—many thanks."

He saw George Courtland looking at him with astonishment.

"This isn't serious, is it?" he asked.

"It isn't anything to worry about," said Dawlish, "but—"

He broke off, for Leven came hurrying down the stairs. He looked neither right nor left, but approached Dawlish, and when he was close, he said stiffly:

"Come upstairs, will you?"

Felicity came hurrying out of the drawing-room, and the trio went upstairs, Dawlish first, Leven behind him as if to make sure that he did not turn to run away, and Felicity bringing up the rear.

The door of the main bedroom was open.

Dawlish saw that a corner of the carpet, near the window, was rolled back. A policeman in uniform was on his knees beside it, and seemed to be unscrewing part of the floor-boards. Dawlish's heart missed a beat. Felicity pushed past Leven and gripped his hand.

Trivett was watching the sergeant, and on the Yard man's face there was an expression of helpless bewilderment. The sergeant worked steadily, and Dawlish, pushing his way past the bed so that he could see more clearly, saw that the floor-board was cut, and screwed down securely; the sergeant had taken out three screws; there were three left.

"This is a new one on me," Dawlish said, curiosity for a moment overlaying a growing unease.

"Is it?" asked Leven, coldly.

Dawlish bit on a sharp retort. It would be folly to lose his temper; the situation would only be worsened. But he felt furiously angry, with himself as much as with anyone else. He had not known that a board had been cut, although, as the sergeant unfastened the last screw and lifted the board, it was obvious that the cut was a recent one. Someone had come into the room, taken a board up, cut it, and so made a hiding-place between the joists.

Trivett looked at Dawlish, as if to say: "What *is* this, Pat?"

Dawlish thought: "In two minutes, he'll be convinced." He grinned, as Leven exclaimed:

"Is there anything there?"

"Yes, sir," said the sergeant, and took out a small black tin box, which Dawlish recognised at once; he had always kept personal papers in it.

The sergeant added: "It's locked, sir."

"Force it," said Trivett, sharply.

"Use the key," said Dawlish, and took a key-case out of his pocket. Then he had another shock; the key of the box wasn't there. That alarmed him more than anything else.

"Force it," repeated Trivett.

It was not difficult; in less than a minute the lid sprang back, revealing the fire and flash of jewels.

Chapter 21

SUSPICION

Trivett let out a long, slow breath.

Felicity's fingers tightened on Dawlish's hand.

Leven shot a single, triumphant glance at Dawlish, and then moved to get a clearer view of the contents of the box.

No one spoke.

Dawlish watched as Leven took the box, and then Trivett startled them all by saying sharply:

"Don't finger it too much!"

Leven started, and dropped the box. Jewels fell out, in a cascade of beauty and light, scattering to the floor.

Felicity turned and looked at Dawlish.

"Not a bad trick," he said, evenly. "One might think I was going to make you a birthday present, my sweet!"

"*You* may think this is funny—" Leven began.

"That's enough," said Trivett, curtly. "Sergeant, be careful how you handle that box, and take it into Haslemere to test for prints." For the moment he usurped Leven's authority, but the local man did not utter a protest. "Telephone as soon as you've finished."

"Very good, sir."

Trivett went down on one knee. He began to help Leven pick up the jewels. They had all been taken out of their setting; diamonds, pearls, emeralds and sapphires, a few lesser gems, but, in all, a collection of great value. Dawlish, who knew a great deal about precious stones, thought it probable that everything which had been stolen after the ball was in that room.

"I think that's the lot," said Trivett.

"And enough, too," murmured Dawlish.

Trivett looked at him steadily.

Dawlish grinned. "Bill, jerk yourself out of it! I didn't know the things were there."

Trivett looked at Leven, seemed to hesitate, and then said slowly:

"I don't for a moment think you did, Pat, but can you prove it?"

There were three sets of finger-prints on the black box. Dawlish's, which were rather faint, Leven's and the police sergeant's. Anyone else who had handled it had done so with gloves. When that news came through, it seemed to Dawlish that no matter how he hated the thought and no matter how reluctant Trivett would be, the police would have to detain him. The story that someone had planted the jewels there might have given Trivett an excuse for taking no immediate action had there been any other finger-prints; but the trick had been cleverly arranged, and there seemed no way out.

Leven had left Trivett in no doubt as to what he thought should be done. It was, in any case, his district, therefore his was the authority, Trivett being there only in an advisory capacity.

Leven had been busy in other directions.

He had forced from Percy an admission that he had been at Lady Fripp's house on the previous afternoon, and the fact that Dawlish had kept that information from the police suggested a degree of complicity which, in the circumstances, could not be ignored. Dawlish realised that it was useless, now, to rely on his reputation, or to remind Trivett that he had kept similar pieces of news back on countless occasions. The weight of evidence was against him, and must be taken into account.

George Courtland, after a talk with Mary Keen, had left; the news would be everywhere in the district before that night was out.

Dawlish was now in the sitting-room, alone with Felicity. A policeman stood outside the door and another was stationed ostentatiously near the window. Upstairs, Alderney and his wife were together, and Mary was in the kitchen with Chloe. Percy was sitting in a police car, a picture of dejection.

"Well, darling," said Felicity.

Dawlish forced a laugh.

"Not so good! But we mustn't go completely mad and assume the worst, you know. Tim and Ted will soon get cracking. You won't get a lot of help from Leven or the local police, but Bill will do everything he can, in the circumstances."

"But what can Tim and Ted do?" asked Felicity.

Dawlish said slowly:

"This is the line I would follow myself. There *is* a single thread connecting all that has happened. It looks as if Alderney, after making a confession about part of what he was doing, actually played a fuller part—I mean, the story about being blackmailed is probably untrue, he was probably working on our sympathy and planning to switch this on to me. Work on Alderney. Find out, if you can, where Alderney and Percy Fripp met, look for this man Paterson, and, as far as the newspapers go, get them to play up the absurdity of it. For once," added Dawlish, with an odd little laugh, "I'd like the newspapers to beat the big drums and tell the world what a wonderful fellow I am!"

Felicity said slowly: "I don't see—"

"You don't see that anything I've suggested will help," said Dawlish. "Yet I—" he broke off, and flung himself into an easy chair. "Of *all* times, I won't be able to do anything myself! I'm hamstrung, and I can think of a dozen things I'd like to do. Tim and Ted—"

"Pat," said Felicity.

"Hm-hm?"

"You know as well as I do that without you, Tim and Ted won't be able to do much."

After a long pause, Dawlish said slowly:

"No. It's up to you."

"I don't think I'm capable of doing much, either," said Felicity. "I—but this won't do! It's madness, Pat! They haven't arrested you yet, you'll be able to work for yourself, you must find a way, you—"

"Steady," said Dawlish.

Felicity stopped.

There was a tap at the door, and Trivett came in alone.

Both of them knew why he had come; before he uttered a word, they knew that he was going to say that a charge was inevitable. He did not speak at once, but looked from one to the other, with a rather dazed expression. Then, to their surprise, he smiled.

"Of course, it's a crazy business," he said.

"Thanks," said Dawlish.

"But you do see the spot I'm in, don't you?"

"Of course I do," said Dawlish, handsomely.

"I'm not going to prefer a charge," said Trivett. "I've persuaded Leven that all we need do is to take you into Haslemere for questioning. And everything that can be done will be done, Pat. I—oh, confound it! It just doesn't make sense!"

"It makes very good sense," Dawlish said. "What crook wouldn't send someone else to jail to save himself?"

Trivett said slowly:

"That isn't quite all."

"What do you mean?" asked Felicity, quickly.

Trivett saw his mistake then, but he had gone too far to withdraw. Dawlish had seen an obvious thing which he believed Felicity had missed; and he had wanted her to remain unaware of it for as long as possible. Now as she looked from him to Trivett, the truth dawned on her. She had been upset before, but now she lost every vestige of colour. She sat down abruptly, as if her legs had suddenly become too weak to support her.

"Darling," said Dawlish, crossing to her side, "Bill isn't a great one on tact, but you would have seen this sooner or later. It's probably better for it to come out now. There *is* a murder charge—a charge of multiple murder—lurking round the corner. And Bill won't miss a half-chance of swinging this in some other quarter."

"I will not," said Trivett.

"It all looks so—damning," said Felicity, in a low-pitched voice. Then she jumped up. "But it won't last," she exclaimed, "it can't last!"

"My sentiments exactly," said Dawlish.

A moment later, she was in his arms . . .

Soon, with a feeling of absolute unreality, he was walking towards the police car, where Percy was sitting, with a police-sergeant by his side and Leven just behind him. It hurt him, that at such a moment, he had to leave Felicity on her own. She could expect no comfort from the Alderneys, none from Percy, none, he supposed, from Mary Keen.

The police driver let in the clutch, but did not at first notice an old Austin which was coming, somewhat erratically, along the road from the village. Just in time to avert a crash he jammed on the brakes, and they came to a dead halt.

Lady Fripp's car, for such it was, was half-way between the road and the drive gates. There was a crashing noise as she tried to change gear. The Austin's engine cut out, and Lady Fripp leaned back in exasperation.

"You'll have to go back," she declared, in a high-pitched voice.

"I don't think that will be necessary," said Leven, who was sitting behind Dawlish. "If you will reverse—"

"If I could reverse, I would," snapped Lady Fripp. "I can make it go forward but not backwards. *You* will have to go back. I—" she broke off. "Good-afternoon, Major Dawlish."

"Hallo," smiled Dawlish. "My wife—"

He stopped when he saw Lady Fripp's expression. She looked at the uniformed driver and then at Leven, and finally turned her gaze towards Dawlish. Her voice was icy.

"Where are you going, Major Dawlish?"

"I'm afraid—" began Leven.

She cut him short.

"I was addressing Major Dawlish." When no one made any immediate response, she added sharply: "I have been told that Major Dawlish finds himself under some suspicion."

"He does," said Leven.

"And are you a party to this nonsense, Chief Inspector?" asked Lady Fripp, icily.

Leven looked his exasperation.

"Stevens, reverse Lady Fripp's car and then drive us out," he said. He was stubbornly determined not to reverse along the narrow drive. "I must remind you, Lady Fripp, that all police business is confidential."

Lady Fripp sniffed.

"I should tell that to the newspapers," she said. "Major Dawlsh, are you under arrest?"

"Next door to it," said Dawlish. "I wonder if you will look after Felicity?" He was relieved at meeting the old woman; from the first, in spite of her oddness, he had liked the sparkle in her eyes; and if they were frosty now, it was because she was angry with the police.

The driver was standing by the side of her car, but she made no attempt to get out.

"Young man," she said, "I do not intend to allow you to take my place, and I will remind you that you are forcing me to block the road. When you have reversed along the drive you may leave, without Major Dawlish. The absurdity of it!"

"My lady—" began Leven, ominously.

"I have some information," said Lady Fripp, "which I feel sure will affect even your obstinacy."

Percy, behind Dawlish, uttered a sharp exclamation.

Lady Fripp glared at him.

Dawlish wondered whether she meant what she said, or whether she was forcing Leven to go back out of sheer perversity. Something would have to happen, and soon, for there came a long toot on a car horn. Dawlish looked towards the village road and saw George Courtland at the wheel of his small car.

Then Courtland blew a longer blast on his horn and, when he knew he had gained their attention, shouted authoritatively:

"Be careful! Keep Lady Fripp out of the way!"

"What does he say?" asked Percy, in tremulous voice.

"Keep Lady Fripp—" echoed Leven.

There was the sound of another car engine, coming from the opposite direction. The harsh noise of changing gear was followed by a squeal of brakes.

"Stevens, tell that driver—" began Leven.

"Look out!" cried Dawlish.

He saw the thing coming through the air—a Mills bomb, judging from the shape of it, a tiny black object against the blue of the sky. He did not notice that the car which had just arrived was already reversing. His eye was on the bomb, falling, falling, until it hit the ground between the hedge and Lady Fripp's car.

"Get out!" yelled Dawlish to Lady Fripp, and as he shouted he prepared to leap. Percy, however, with the tenacity of a badly frightened man clutched his legs, and would not let him go. The fuse of the bomb, burning steadily, was easily seen. If it went off, there would be no chance at all for the old woman in the car.

Shaking off Percy's frenzied grip, Dawlish sprang forward, scooped it up, and tossed it into the air. Then he turned and flung himself to the ground; and as he did so, the bomb went off.

Chapter 22

"ALL ABOARD"

Dawlish got slowly to his feet.

Smoke still hovered about the hedge and the cars, filling his lungs. One window of the Austin was shattered; there were small holes in the roof. Leven was standing by the driver's door, talking urgently to Lady Fripp.

"I tell you I am all right!" exclaimed the old woman, peevishly. "I am a little deaf, that is all."

Dawlish caught a glimpse of Stevens, leaning against the front of the police car. There was blood on his forehead. Percy, white-faced, sat where he was, shivering violently.

Dawlish became aware that George Courtland was yelling at him.

He turned abruptly.

"Come on, Dawlish!"

Courtland had managed to squeeze his car between the back of the Austin and the hedge. Further along the road, the car from which the bomb had been thrown was reversing in a gateway.

If he went with George, Dawlish thought quickly, the worst possible construction would be put on the move by the police.

On the other hand, the weight of evidence was already so heavily against him that the situation would hardly be worsened.

He jumped forward.

"Hold tight!" cried George.

His eyes were glistening as if he were enjoying this adventure. Suspicions of George loomed large in Dawlish's mind, but he had committed himself, and there was nothing else he could do now. He remembered Leven's scorn when it had been suggested that the Courtlands were implicated.

The little two-seater was travelling at great speed in the wake of a low-built car in front of them. The distance between them was a little more than a hundred yards, and for the first two or three minutes the gap neither shortened nor increased. Dawlish clambered behind George, and, with careful manoeuvring, managed to lower himself into the seat next to the driver. Legroom was limited, and he sat with his knees almost touching his chin, watching the car ahead.

Questions were flooding his mind—about the attack on Lady Fripp and about George's warning. What had George learned, and how had he learned it? There was little doubt that his warning cry had saved the little group of people by the gate from complete disaster.

What had Lady Fripp come to say?

All doubt that she had been talking to impress Leven was gone; its importance must have been great indeed to cause such a risky attack.

Both cars skirted Haslemere.

Dawlish thought the assailants were going to take the Godalming Road, where they could move more quickly. Instead, they took a by-road, a twisting and turning lane which led to Hindhead.

He wished he were armed.

He looked at George, who was concentrating on his driving. The younger man had a set smile and still gave the impression that he was enjoying this himself. He glanced at Dawlish, and his grin widened.

Dawlish said: "What brought you?"

George negotiated a tricky turn before he answered.

"The whole set-up. Especially you!" He did not look round. "I'm not a stranger to the district, you know, although I've been away a few years."

"I know," said Dawlish.

"And Lady Fripp, bless her, has always had a soft spot for me," said George. "I had a chat with her after the shindy there the other night. Nothing much came of it, except that I was acquainted with the general situation. And when I realised you were likely to be put in the lock-up at any time, I went to have a word with her. She is the type who can move mountains. And I was followed," George added.

Dawlish's interest quickened.

"I didn't let on that I'd twigged it," George told him, watching the bright streak of the other car. "I talked to the old dame in her drawing-room, with the window wide open. The fellows were outside, listening. She went off the deep end. Policemen without an ounce of sense and all that kind of thing—did you know that her frosty approval rests on you, too?"

"No," said Dawlish.

"Well, it does—and how! Partly, I think, because you're championing her nephew. In spite of all she says, she wished that bygones could be bygones. He's her only relative, you know."

"Yes," said Dawlish, wishing that George would get to the point.

They were travelling as quickly as the road would allow them, and the other car was still about a hundred yards ahead. By now, the county police would be warned of what had happened, and the car in front might be the first to run into an ambush. There was a touch of unreality about everything that was happening—particularly this drive through the countryside on a glorious warm day, with the air rushing past their faces and George chatting as if they were off to a garden party.

"So she said she'd made a discovery of some importance, and *was* going to tell you about it this afternoon. She asked me to drive her. I declined, pleading urgent business. I didn't tell her what it was, but as soon as she started off in her antediluvian auto, the other customers followed. I followed *them* as far as Alum, and then came the other way round—I thought I might get there first."

"You took a chance," said Dawlish.

"My dear chap, it was the *only* chance. I didn't know what the villains were going to attempt, I did know that they hadn't yet taken action and, presumably, that they were going to wait until she got near *Four Ways*. I thought—well, you know what I thought. And here we are!"

Dawlish smiled, in spite of himself, and then asked:

"Do you know what she discovered?"

"No, she wouldn't tell me. She didn't think it was wise to tell anyone but you and the police. She actually had the nerve to say that she didn't want to lead me into danger!" George laughed. "I had a feeling it was something close at hand," he added. "She was coming away from that other monstrosity of hers, the air-raid shelter, when I arrived. One of her schemes is to pull the place down."

"Yes," said Dawlish, and remembered that Lady Fripp had talked of that to him.

He sat back, with his eyes narrowed.

George's story seemed straightforward enough, but it made

little difference to the actual situation except that Lady Fripp had stumbled across something which she thought would help him in his present plight. George was probably right when he said that it was something near at hand—which meant near her house.

The air-raid shelter.

He remembered his first sight of it, and he remembered Eileen. It was a curious business. Eileen and Percy had been in secret alliance against Lady Fripp—a small thing, but small things might be important.

What had that to do with the air-raid shelter?

"Rather strange how Fripp lost his nerve over the bomb," said George meditatively. "He never was a brave man, but I've seldom seen a bigger panic."

"Danger takes men all ways," said Dawlish. "How did you know who he was?"

"Confound it, man, we were buddies in our childhood! It hit his aunt pretty hard."

"It must have done," said Dawlish.

George cut a corner sharply.

"Look out!" cried Dawlish.

George grinned. "I can handle anything on wheels," he said.

The big car in front of them was sweeping round the wide bend which edged the Punch Bowl. A little way ahead there was a 'road up' sign. Half a dozen men were working in the wake of a steam-roller. A man with a green flag waved the big car on.

"It's slowing down," George said.

They had almost caught up with the big car, and Dawlish guessed what was in George's mind. He planned to try to overtake the runaway, and swing across its front wheels. It would be forced to stop, for the driver dared not take a chance of being pushed over to the left, perhaps down the steep bank of the Punch Bowl itself.

"*Hold tight!*" yelled George.

Dawlish saw the danger as quickly as he.

The big car had jammed on its brakes. George could not turn right, or he would crash into the steam roller. He could not go on, or he would crash into the back of the fugitives' car. Yet if he turned left—

The Punch Bowl seemed to gape in front of them.

George swung left.

There was just room to pass the big car on the nearside—but it would need perfect judgement. The wheels of the little car were within a few inches of the edge of the Bowl. Travelling at speed, the wheels were steady enough, but—

The car lurched.

The ground on the nearside gave way.

One moment they were on the verge; the next they had dropped, and were falling down the side of that steep valley.

Although he had been half prepared for it, it came swiftly enough to take Dawlish by surprise. The engine cut out, as George shouted the one word, "Jump!"

The car was tipping over dangerously. Dawlish knew that if he jumped it might fall on him. He looked downwards; there seemed to be a bottomless pit.

George jumped.

Dawlish felt the car steady for a moment, as if it were going to settle on all four wheels. That was his chance. As he, too, jumped, his foot caught. It was only a temporary check, but enough to alter his direction. He fell heavily, and began to roll slowly down the slope. Unable to stop himself, gathering speed at every yard, he buried his face in his arms. His body seemed alive with pain as he bumped over stones and moving gravel. Down—down—

He hit something which was big enough to slow up his mad gyration; it gave him time to grab at a shrub. It held.

He stayed there, gasping for breath, the sun hot on his back.

He felt sick and his body was wracked with pain, but gradually that eased out. He thought he heard someone call, but could not be sure. He did not look about him, but lay still with his head in the shade of the bush which he had grabbed for safety.

It seemed a long time before he stirred himself and looked downwards.

A great volume of smoke was rising towards the sky.

'George's car,' he thought, vaguely.

The men who had forced them over the edge doubtless saw that fire, and thought they had been completely successful.

Dawlish staggered up.

He could see the flames, now; the skeletal frame of the little car, bare bones that were supposed to have incarcerated his own. He turned away, with a sick feeling, and then he heard a shout.

"*Dawlish!*"

That was George!

"*Hallo, there!*" he called back.

He heard the scrunch of moving gravel as the man came towards him. He walked forward, unprepared for the torn, dishevelled figure which staggered into view.

"Well," said George's voice, jaunty as ever, issuing from a dusty, blackened face, "that was a bit of luck."

"Yes," agreed Dawlish, heavily.

"Two or three wallahs are coming down to lend us a hand," said George. "I'm sorry the other beggars got away. It looks to me as if they had this in mind."

"It's possible," said Dawlish, dryly.

"Well," said George, taking out a battered cigarette, "we tried!" He was smiling, but his eyes were hard—showing his facetiousness to be a façade, behind which he secretly watched, "We'd better get back to your place, hadn't we?"

Dawlish said slowly:

"I don't think so, George. Lady Fripp's house is the next rendezvous."

George raised his eyebrows.

"Why?"

Dawlish shrugged. "If she did learn something there—"

Before he could finish, rescuers appeared, half-a-dozen men who were walking at intervals of a few yards, searching for the 'bodies'. Had Dawlish been in a different mood he would have appreciated the ludicrous expressions on their faces when they saw the two 'victims' standing and talking. But Dawlish appreciated only one thing; one of the men was a policeman.

Leven would doubtless think he had tried to escape.

"Aren't you Mr. Dawlish?" asked the policeman.

"That's right," said Dawlish, and added under his breath: "Here it comes."

"I've just had a message about you, sir," said the policeman. "Will you go to Lady Fripp's house, at once?"

Chapter 23

SHELTER

Greatly relieved, Dawlish attempted to walk back to the road, but the fall had taken more out of him than he realised. Before he had gone a couple of yards, he was forced to accept support.

Once on level ground again someone offered him tea from a thermos flask, liberally laced with whisky. Grateful for it; and much strengthened, he was yet impatient to get to Lady Fripp's house.

It was a quarter of an hour before the policeman had commandeered a car and they were on their way, George sitting by his side. Dawlish's mind was confused, but he clung to one thought; the air-raid shelter, and the fact that Mortimer had been injured as he was going to it. Vividly, Dawlish remembered seeing the man lying on the steps, with his head battered.

They drew near.

"Hal-*lo!*" exclaimed George.

As he spoke, a shot sounded loud and clear above the noise of the engine. But it was not the shot which had made him exclaim—it was the line of police cars near Lady Fripp's house.

There were a dozen of them, perhaps more. Several policemen were standing about.

"What's the trouble?" asked Dawlish, slowly.

"Superintendent Trivett's just inside the grounds, sir," directed one of them.

Dawlish limped towards the gate, aware that whatever was happening was of supreme importance. He heard more shooting. Someone swore. Someone else said:

"We'd better have tear-gas."

"Look out," said the police escort, "it's dangerous just about here, sir."

He was right; a shot rang out, and a bullet screeched above their heads. Dawlish glanced up. The shot had come from the window of Lady Fripp's house, he thought—the first floor. A little way along the drive was a police car, lying on its side. Behind it was Trivett, Leven, and two other men—all of them carrying guns.

Dawlish reached the cover of the car, and George hurried after him.

Trivett glanced round.

"Hallo, Pat," he said. "Been having a dust-bath?"

"You could call it that. What's all this?"

"We've cornered the beggars," Trivett said, "but they're having fun."

"Fun!" echoed George.

Three shots rang out in quick succession, and Trivett's lips tightened.

"Lady Fripp discovered that her air-raid shelter was being used pretty freely," Trivett said, in a calm enough voice. "That was earlier today. As soon as she told us, we came here in strength, and decided to take you on trust, but—"

"Paterson had already taken possession?" suggested Dawlish.

"As far as I can see, all the crooks in the district were summoned, and came hurrying. They've entrenched themselves in the house, and shoot at everyone who pokes his head up too high.

"Not much point in it," said Dawlish.

"They know they can't expect much less than a life sentence," Trivett said, "and they're fighting it out. I'm waiting for tear-gas."

"What about the back way?"

"They've covered all approaches to the house," said Trivett. "There are a couple of dozen of them—we've disturbed the hornet's nest all right." He gave a dry, mirthless chuckle. "Not quite what we expected!"

Dawlish made no comment.

"Surely we can do something," said George.

"Not yet," said Trivett, curtly.

A policeman moved from the car to the road, to take a message, and three shots rang out. He was not touched, but it was a measure of the danger.

"What's in the shelter?" asked George. "Does anyone know?"

"We can guess," said Trivett.

"No, don't tell me!—Jewels?"

"Don't forget that we've been looking for the proceeds of robberies up and down the country over a period of eighteen months. Do you know what I think?"

"No longer," said Dawlish.

"Some of them are going to make a run for it soon," said Trivett, "and they'll try and clear a path with some fast shooting." He looked on edge as he spoke; and the same thought had been in Dawlish's mind. One thing seemed quite certain: unless there were jewels of great value in the house or in the air-raid shelter, these men would not put up such a fight.

But *was* it certain?

Wouldn't they fight because, as Trivett had said, they were cornered and, for the most part, were likely to be convicted of murder, or as accessories to murder?

A sudden thought passed through Dawlish's mind.

"Where's the maid?" he asked.

Trivett shrugged his shoulders. "Inside, I'm afraid. We've had a lot of trouble from Robert Fripp about her."

"Oh," said Dawlish, heavily.

"He wanted to get through to her," said Trivett. "I had to send him away, he was kicking up such a fuss. Sentiment's all right, but—" he broke off, and shrugged.

"*Aren't* we going to attack?" asked George, after a pause.

"All we've got to do for the time being is to make sure the beggars don't get away," said Trivett doggedly. "When reinforcements—"

He broke off.

There was a shout from the road. Next moment, Dawlish saw Percy Fripp dashing across the small lawn in front of the shrubbery. Obviously he had forced his way through the hedge without being observed. Two policemen gave chase. Shooting came, fast and furious, from the house. One policeman fell, but Percy seemed to bear a charmed life. He reached the drive in front of the porch, and leapt towards the steps.

Trivett said in a low-pitched voice:

"He means to see that maid—"

"*Look out!*" someone yelled.

There was a sudden outburst of renewed shooting. Trivett flung caution to the winds, and stood up to see what was happening. Dawlish followed his example. Two or three men were running from the house towards the open fields. Were they quite crazy? Didn't they realise that there was not a chance in a thousand of escape?

Something burst in front of Dawlish.

He smelt the sharp, acrid smell.

Tear-gas!

"Bill—"

Trivett said savagely: "They'll do it!"

The air seemed full of the wispy vapours of the gas; men began to choke and retch sickeningly. Dawlish, holding his breath, backed away from the car. A container of the gas had burst just in front of him. His hands flew to his eyes.

"Get further back," Dawlish muttered.

"They'll get—" began Leven.

A container of tear-gas burst in his face. The shock sent him reeling to the ground. Tear-gas containers were being flung from the windows and by the men who were making their way from the house. The thieves were clearing a path with it, and if they went on at this rate, they would be able to take what cars they liked to get away.

Dawlish reached the road. A policeman was spluttering wildly, but still had his wits about him.

"Drive as many cars off as you can," snapped Dawlish, "make a barrier across the road, and—"

He stopped, for a container hit the car by which he was standing. There was nothing he could do to save himself. Blinded, he gulped the foul stuff in, the fit of coughing wracking his whole body.

He was vaguely aware of men passing him.

He heard an engine start up, and a car move off.

Three cars were stolen from those parked outside the house, and in all six men escaped. The alarm was not raised until the cars were a long way from Grayshott and, within two hours, all three cars were found, abandoned.

That was after the reinforcements had arrived at Lady Fripp's.

They made short work of the remaining thieves, and the prisoners were lodged in an empty house near Haslemere.

Nobody, now, was disposed to suspect Dawlish of complicity, and for this he was duly thankful.

Lady Fripp's discovery of the use to which her shelter was being put had helped to clear him of suspicion. Dawlish heard her story again from Trivett. It was amplified by the fact that they had been able to see over the shelter. Obviously it had been used for some time. A few jewels were still there—they had been stored, it proved, in a small wall safe, the door of which was standing open. There were camp beds, a few chairs, stocks of cigarettes and a store of food. One of the men who had been caught had talked freely. The thieves who lodged in various houses in the district had gone to the shelter for instructions from time to time.

He said more.

Paterson, who had been one of the men to escape in the tear-gas attack, had been preparing for another onslaught on the houses in the district. Mortimer had been killed because, being chief custodian of the jewels, he had used his knowledge as a threat and demanded a larger share of the profits. Jewels were brought in frequently, others were taken out and sold.

Alderney's story was confirmed in every detail.

None of the men appeared to know anything about the hiding of jewels at *Four Ways*. Dawlish did not think they would have kept such knowledge back. Paterson had probably arranged the frame-up, but one thing was evident: Dawlish looked at Trivett as the thought passed through his mind.

"Well, Bill, someone who was often at *Four Ways* made the hole in the floor and did his stuff."

"The same someone poisoned Alderney," said Trivett.

"I wish I could think why," Leven said.

Dawlish rubbed the bridge of his nose.

"Shall we say revenge? Alderney had made things difficult for Paterson and his employer, hadn't he? Alderney was no further use. If he could be poisoned in my house, and the jewels were found there later, I would be held responsible, and the real murderer would be safe in retirement."

"Who—" began Leven.

"My dear chap!" protested Dawlish, "there's only one candidate for the honour. I was the biggest fool," he added, and laughed mirthlessly. "I took him on trust because of his innocent blue eyes!"

"You mean—*Fripp?*"

"Of course," said Dawlish quietly. "Little Percy, who rushed into the house to save his Eileen. Rather remarkable, don't you think, that he was allowed to get in when the policemen who followed him were picked off? Remarkable, too, that he was so frightened by the bomb, that he tried to stop me flinging it away. Percy didn't want Lady Fripp alive. He guessed what she had found out, you see, and it would have suited his book to let her die."

Trivett said: "I wonder if you're right."

"Oh, I'm right enough," said Dawlish, "if only by a process of elimination. Where is he, by the way?"

"At *Four Ways*," said Trivett.

"I hope you're sure," Dawlish murmured.

Trivett smiled. "I doubt whether he will realise that anyone suspects him yet. You know, Pat, you haven't got any real evidence."

"I don't think it will be long before we get it," said Dawlish. "It's clear enough, that Eileen, the maid, had some idea—and was bribed to keep silent. She was friendly to Percy Fripp—he told me that himself." He laughed a little. "Oh, it's clever!"

Then he saw that Trivett and Leven were staring at him fixedly. His voice dropped. "Now what's the matter?" he asked. "Afraid of questioning Eileen?"

"We *can't* question Eileen."

"She was shot," said Leven, soberly.

"According to Percy, by a police bullet," added Trivett, in a low-pitched voice.

"*Now* we know why he rushed in to see her," said Dawlish, after a pause. "He had to stop Eileen's mouth at all costs." He stood up. "Well we'd better have a go at him, hadn't we?"

It was as they were driving towards *Four Ways* that he remembered the morphine with which Alderney had been drugged; and he suggested that they should search the garage.

Chapter 24

PERCY

When Dawlish and the two detectives arrived, Percy was sitting on his bed in the living room above the garage. His shoes were off, and he was wriggling his toes, the picture of child-like innocence. Outside, two policemen stood, tall and immovable, to make sure he did not get away.

He looked up with a shy smile.

"Percy," Dawlish said gruffly, "the game's up."

"The—*game*?"

"Perhaps we shouldn't call it a game," said Dawlish. He watched the little man carefully. He had to admire his brazenness and his presence of mind. He thought of the murderous attack on Percy in this room. That incident alone had seemed to prove that Percy was blameless.

In fact, Dawlish reasoned, that incident was one of the keys to the mystery.

"I must confess that I don't quite understand you," Percy said, softly.

"You're going to," said Dawlish.

"You surely don't suspect *me*," said Percy, his voice pitched perhaps, a little higher than usual. "Why, you yourself saved my life when I was attacked by these villains, Mr. Dawlish!" He smiled at Trivett. "I do assure you, gentlemen, that Mr. Dawlish is seriously mistaken if he suspects *me* of complicity. You surely understand that, as I have been in prison for so long, these plans, these operations, were going on when I was in no position to assist."

Trivett said nothing. Leven looked out of the window.

"As you say, it goes back quite a way," said Dawlish, "to the time before you were sent to prison. As long ago as that, this campaign of robbery was in existence, although not on such a large scale. You and Roland Mortimer were the leaders, Percy."

"You joke, Mr. Dawlish."

"And Mortimer decided," Dawlish continued, inexorably, "that you were in his way. So, he framed you on the embezzlement charge. He went to your office and told you what he had done, knowing that the only way you could save yourself from the charge of embezzlement was to admit the truth about being a receiver of stolen jewels. He knew you would keep quiet. And you did, Percy. Do you remember telling me, that prisons were a breeding-ground for crime? That many criminals laid their plans for future activities inside those four walls?"

Percy did not speak; he had lost a little of his colour.

"You laid plans, also. Because, although Mortimer didn't realise it, you had a reliable contact—none other that Paterson, who escaped with most of the jewels today. Paterson isn't known locally, but the police knew the locality was suspect, and you tried to heighten suspicion of Alderney by telling me a local man was concerned. Oh, you've worked hard, even warning me when I first went to Lady Fripp's house, with a shout which seemed to prove your friendship. In fact, of course, no local celebrity is concerned. You created one."

"What an imagination!" murmured Percy.

"Paterson looked after your interests," Dawlish continued. "You sent messages out through carefully picked warders, and through prisoners who were inside on short term sentences. So, you knew the exact position. Roland Mortimer, to his mortification, found that Paterson was the strong man of the outfit. Paterson, you see, could have told the truth about the embezzlement story, and Mortimer preferred to accept a minor position in the organisation sooner than go to prison. But he planned revenge, Percy. One of the first things he did, when you came out, for instance, was to send two of his friends to attack you here. All the time, he planned to take over from the leader, Paterson, and prevent you from really asserting your authority again.

"When Alderney made trouble, Mortimer had a wonderful chance. The jewels had to be taken away, but could not be taken far. The air-raid shelter at Lady Fripp's house was a perfect hiding-place. He persuaded members of the organisation to take them there. You didn't like the situation at all, Percy, and, on the day when I went to see Lady Fripp, you went to see Roland Mortimer. You arranged, also, for others to be at hand in case your attack failed. Mortimer knew that you wanted to get into the shelter. He rushed there; once inside, he would have been fairly safe. You reached him first and attacked him, knowing that the men hiding in the grounds would shoot him, and so re-established your ascendancy. Doesn't this make an interesting story?"

"Most interesting," Percy said, shrilly. "If there were a word of truth in it, I would be most alarmed. What a villain you make me out to be!"

"A very far-seeing one," said Dawlish, "for you learnt my habits from your friends in jail. To counteract any chance that the police might ask me to help, you attempted to scare me away by having Flash Ben's body hung from my roof. When that didn't work, you appealed to my, and my wife's, sympathy in order to stay at *Four Ways*."

"I am going to appeal to it again," Percy said, "and—"

"Later," said Dawlish, curtly. "You then saw a way of framing me, Percy, and killing Alderney at the same time. Neat revenge in both cases, and, if it came off, you would be free. You also arranged that I should be suspected of the kidnapping of Lady Alderney."

"Isn't she really Mrs. Keen?" asked Percy, gently. "After all, if anything *should* happen to me, the truth about Alderney is bound to come out. You're far too good-natured to allow that to happen." He smiled.

Dawlish smiled in turn.

"I think Alderney can take it," he said. "He may lose a title and position, but he's got his wife and his daughter."

"I—see." Percy looked at Trivett. "Superintendent, you are a shrewd officer. You have heard of such a thing as *evidence*, haven't you? You may agree with these rather highly coloured accusations against me, but it would be a different matter to *prove* it, would it not? I wonder if you would give me a cigarette, Mr. Dawlish."

Dawlish took out his case and tossed it to him.

"How kind," murmured Percy. "It is all arrant nonsense, of course. I deny every word of it." He tossed the case back, and Dawlish caught it.

"It won't help you," said Dawlish.

"Indeed?"

"Three people knew the truth about you," Dawlish went on. "Eileen, whom you murdered in cold blood this afternoon—"

"*Murdered!* What an extraordinary idea. In fact I rushed through a hail of bullets to save her!"

"Mortimer, whom you arranged to have murdered," went on Dawlish, in a hard voice, "and Paterson, who, no doubt in consequence of some oversight on your part, is still alive."

Percy drew deeply on the cigarette.

"I don't know a man named Paterson."

"He knows you," said Dawlish. "People are often loyal Percy, but there are some things which put too great a strain on loyalty. Paterson discovered that when he was caught on the road an hour ago."

Percy sat absolutely still.

"With the jewels," Trivett said, sharply.

"He—" began Percy, and then he broke off. He smiled, a slow, gentle smile. "Oh, no," he said. "Such a simple bluff won't help you, Mr. Dawlish. Bring the man in! Let me see him! Let me deny any charge he brings against me!"

Trivett turned to Leven, and nodded.

Dawlish watched the little man on the bed steadily. The next ten minutes would be crucial. No one knew where Paterson was; the bluff might work, or it might not.

"I hope he won't be long," said Percy.

"He won't," said Dawlish. "There are one or two trimmings to my story, Percy. The log which fell on Mrs. Arbor's foot, and kept her away, so that you had to help in the kitchen, the morphine which you were able to put in Alderney's coffee."

Dawlish glanced towards the door. "Are they coming?"

"I'll see," said Trivett.

He went to the door and opened it, looked out, and then turned round and said with a cheerful smile:

"Yes, they've just left the house."

A loud voice sounded outside—Ted Beresford's voice.

"Hallo, Leven, who are you taking up there?"

Leven's answer was inaudible; but Ted's words seemed to do

more to worry Percy than anything else had done. He jumped off the bed, and rushed to the window. Dawlish let him go, knowing he could not see who was outside. Percy drew back—and then slipped two fingers into his pocket. As Percy put his hand to his mouth, Dawlish leaped forward and knocked it away.

Three little white tablets fell to the ground.

Suddenly the door opened and Leven came in. Dawlish could not see his face, but he knew at once that something of importance had happened.

"*It's all right—we have got Paterson!*" cried Leven.

Paterson had been caught after a trivial mishap. He had been driving a car with two sets of number plates, and a watchful policeman had noticed it when he was held up at cross-roads, and questioned him.

Dawlish was more than satisfied with the consequences of the subsequent arrest, for Paterson, once he had realised there was no hope, had talked freely. There were a few details to add, but the story Dawlish had pieced together was right in almost every particular.

Tired, triumphant, a little sad, Dawlish had returned to *Four Ways*.

Mary Keen had gone back to London, but was to return to live at *Akers*. Alderney, having made his peace with Dawlish, said that whatever publicity he got, whatever happened, he was going to stick it out at Haslemere; and Janice agreed that it was the right thing to do.

They were all gathered together in the drawing-room of *Four Ways*, helping Felicity as she poured out coffee.

George Courtland had arrived before dinner, hoping that he was not in the way. He had run Mary to the station, he said, and now felt at a loose end. True, he had come in at the middle of the show but hoped he deserved to hear the final story.

He heard it . . .

"They kept off violence for a long time," Trivett wound up, in this last exposition. "The first murder was almost accidental. After that, of course, they were in line for a capital charge. Then followed the liquidation of Flash Ben, and after that the attack on Mortimer. It's apparent, now, that there were two factions among the thieves—Mortimer's and Paterson's, and Percy was keeping away for the time being, leaving Paterson to do the dirty work. Mortimer's position was fairly powerful, you know—and, with a few strong-arm merchants he could protect himself. He was killed, while rushing to the air-raid shelter to get help from his men. Three of them were downstairs at the time—if we'd had the wit to look in the shelter, we might have stopped the final attempt to get away."

Lady Fripp sniffed.

"*If* you'd had the wit," she said.

Dawlish chuckled; and she looked at him with a twinkle in her eyes.

"Give the police their due," he pleaded. "They did a fair job."

"I will grant that," said Lady Fripp. She finished her coffee, and looked at George. "Perhaps this time you will drive me home," she suggested. "It will be a change for the Dawlish's to have their house to themselves for a little while."

The Alderneys left soon afterwards. Dawlish and Felicity stood on the porch and watched them drive off. Trivett followed, and later—much later—Ted and Tim, who had come together, set off for London.

The house was very quiet.

"All over," murmured Dawlish.

"It could have been a lot worse," said Felicity.

Dawlish put his arm about her waist, and they strolled round the garden. The perfume of night-scented stock filled the air, and they stood near it, looking at the tiny white flowers which were just visible in the darkness.

"Thoughtful?" he suggested.

"I wish I hadn't taken such a liking to Percy," Felicity said, and then forced a laugh. "Let's forget it!"

But Dawlish knew that it would be a long time before they did forget.

About the Author

John Creasey, born in 1908, was a paramount English crime and science fiction writer who used myriad pseudonyms for more than six hundred novels. He founded the UK Crime Writers' Association in 1953. In 1962, his book *Gideon's Fire* received the Edgar Award for Best Novel from the Mystery Writers of America. Many of the characters featured in Creasey's titles became popular, including George Gideon of Scotland Yard, who was the basis for a subsequent television series and film. Creasey died in Salisbury, UK, in 1973.